"Put down your weapon."

Ignoring Nelson's words, Mia asked, "If you're not with them, who are you?"

Before he could answer, another barrage of gunfire rent the air, this time the bullets definitely directed at them. Nelson grabbed the gun in Mia's hand.

More bullets whizzed past his head. He hooked an arm around the woman's shoulders, taking her to the ground, as he said to Diesel, "Belly."

The dog immediately dropped to lie flat in the dirt.

He aimed toward the last muzzle flash he'd seen and fired. The sound of somebody crashing through the forest echoed in the stillness.

Rocky Mountain K-9 Unit

*These police officers fight for justice
with the help of their brave canine partners.*

Terri Reed's romance and romantic suspense novels have appeared on the *Publishers Weekly* top twenty-five and NPD BookScan top one hundred lists and have been featured in *USA TODAY*, *Christian Fiction* magazine and *RT Book Reviews*. Her books have been finalists for the Romance Writers of America RITA® Award and the National Readers' Choice Award and finalists three times for the American Christian Fiction Writers Carol Award. Contact Terri at terrireed.com or PO Box 19555, Portland, OR 97224.

Books by Terri Reed

Love Inspired Suspense

Buried Mountain Secrets
Secret Mountain Hideout
Christmas Protection Detail
Secret Sabotage

Rocky Mountain K-9 Unit

Detection Detail

Alaska K-9 Unit

Alaskan Rescue

True Blue K-9 Unit: Brooklyn

Explosive Situation

True Blue K-9 Unit

Seeking the Truth

Visit the Author Profile page at LoveInspired.com for more titles.

DETECTION DETAIL

TERRI REED

LOVE INSPIRED SUSPENSE
INSPIRATIONAL ROMANCE

Special thanks and acknowledgment are given to Terri Reed for her contribution to the Rocky Mountain K-9 Unit miniseries.

LOVE INSPIRED® SUSPENSE

INSPIRATIONAL ROMANCE

ISBN-13: 978-1-335-72299-7

Recycling programs
for this product may
not exist in your area.

Detection Detail

Copyright © 2022 by Harlequin Books S.A.

For questions and comments about the quality of this book, please contact us at CustomerService@Harlequin.com.

Love Inspired
22 Adelaide St. West, 41st Floor
Toronto, Ontario M5H 4E3, Canada
www.LoveInspired.com

Printed in U.S.A.

The fear of the Lord is the beginning of wisdom:
and the knowledge of the holy is understanding.
—*Proverbs* 9:10

Thank you to Emily Rodmell and Tina James
for all your support. I'm grateful to have you on my side.

Thank you to the other authors
in the Rocky Mountain K-9 Unit: Valerie Hansen,
Laura Scott, Dana Mentink, Jodie Bailey,
Elizabeth Goddard, Maggie K. Black, Lynette Eason,
Lenora Worth and Katy Lee. It's always enjoyable
to brainstorm ideas and plot points with you all.
It makes the writing fun!

ONE

Officer Nelson Rivers puzzled over the mysterious car fire he and his accelerant detection dog, a yellow Lab named Diesel, had recently worked. An unconscious, unidentified victim. A possible missing baby. Who set the fire and why?

So many questions. He hoped the forensic team would be able to provide answers at this morning's briefing.

He turned into the parking lot of the Rocky Mountain K-9 Unit headquarters, located on the outskirts of Denver. The sizable campus also housed the FBI K-9 training center. The two-story building, made of redbrick and beige shingles, was dwarfed by the Rockies in the distance. An American flag mounted on a pole flapped over the front entrance in the cool April morning breeze.

He parked in his usual spot, then led Diesel to the entrance, where he used his access code to enter the building.

He waved to Jodie Chen, assistant to their boss, Sergeant Tyson Wilkes, on his way to the conference room. Adjacent to Jodie's office was Tyson's large, glass-encased office, but Nelson could see the sergeant and the other K-9 unit members already assembling for the Monday morning meeting in the huge, glass-walled conference room, the center piece of the first floor.

After settling Diesel in his kennel next to Nelson's desk, he headed into the conference room. He took a seat next to his army ranger buddy, K-9 handler Ben Sawyer.

Ben clapped him on the back. Over six feet of muscled rancher turned lawman, Ben always had a bit of scruff on his face and in his attitude. He hailed from Wyoming and dressed the part with well-worn jeans, a chambray shirt and a Stetson covering his dark hair. After his service with the army, he'd been a K-9 handler with the Wyoming State Police K-9 Unit. Then Tyson had recruited him to the RMKU when he began the unit six months ago.

Ben's partner, a Doberman named Shadow, excelled in protection and apprehension. "Heard you caught a fire," Ben drawled.

"That we did," Nelson replied, stretching out his legs beneath the oblong wooden table. As the only arson detection team in the unit, he and Diesel had deployed Friday night to a fire near the entrance to the Rocky Mountain State Park.

It wasn't unusual for any of the K-9 teams of the RMKU to be deployed for various different emergencies. They were under contract for the year to the FBI to serve as a mobile response unit assisting authorities on cases within the diverse and far-reaching terrain of the Rocky Mountain region. If all went well, their unit would become a permanent addition to the FBI. There was never a dull moment on the job, and Nelson loved it.

"Was it bad?" The question came from Harlow Zane, originally from the Santa Fe K-9 Unit, seated across the table. She and her partner, a female beagle named Nell, specialized in cadaver detection.

"Nobody dead on scene. One unconscious victim." Nelson's gut clenched with dread. "Possible missing baby."

Frowning, Harlow smoothed back a wayward strand of blond hair from her bun. "Good and bad, then."

"Should we head out there?" Lucas Hudson asked from a few seats down. He and his dog, Angel, a female border collie, handled search and rescue and had come to the team along with Nelson from the Idaho State Police K-9 Unit.

From the front of the room, their boss, Tyson, answered, "At this point there is no evidence beyond an empty car seat to suggest a missing child." Tyson met Nelson's gaze. "Nelson, tell us what you and Diesel discovered."

Nelson rose. "We arrived on scene to find a car on fire, a midsize sedan, but thankfully the wildland fire management team had the blaze under control. The accelerant used was denatured alcohol, a clear colorless ethanol deliberately infused with hard-to-separate lethal substances meant to keep people from digesting the liquid. It's normally used as a solvent, a cleaning agent and even a pest exterminator. Highly flammable, and when ignited, water is ineffective in putting out the flames. The wildland fire team used specialized foam to douse the blaze."

A murmur of surprise rippled through the room.

"From the direction the car faced, the driver most likely was coming from the park," Nelson continued. "Black tire marks crisscrossed the asphalt, suggesting the driver had lost control of the vehicle. Icy roads in April aren't uncommon, especially at the higher elevations."

Tyson taped up a photo of a woman with curly, short brown hair and hazel eyes on the glass wall beside him. "This is our victim, who is in a coma. The Boulder PD have identified her as Kate Montgomery, a wildlife artist from here in Denver. Single. No children. We are operating on the assumption she was driving the car since the vehicle was registered to her."

Nelson nodded agreement. "However, an infant car seat had been flung on its side farther down the road and a pale pink baby blanket lay nearby, along with the unconscious victim." Nelson frowned at the memory. "There were no signs of an infant in the vicinity." He and the officers on scene had searched. "But there were drops of the accelerant and tire tracks fifty feet from the burning car."

"It certainly seems like some sort of abduction," Daniella Vargas said. Her ebony eyes held a grim expression. The tough, no-nonsense woman, who'd joined the team from the Montana State Police K-9 Unit, was a bit of loner. Her dog, a Malinois named Zara, was a fierce protection dog. "But they obviously didn't want to kill Miss Montgomery."

"Or they believed they had," offered Reece Campbell. The former Denver K-9 Unit officer and his male German shepherd, Maverick, were the best crime scene detection duo around.

"Paramedics had to use lifesaving measures on the victim," Nelson told the group, confirming Reece's suspicion.

"Which explains the coma," Chris Fuller stated dryly, as he folded himself into a chair at the end of the table.

The former Phoenix K-9 officer sported a scar over his left eyebrow. Nelson had never asked the brooding man how he'd obtained it. Ben would know. However, Nelson chose to stay out of the tension between the two half siblings. Chris and his dog, Teddy, a spaniel, specialized in tracking, had an impressive record that had helped Ben convince Tyson to bring his half brother on the team.

"Indeed," Tyson said. Turning back to the glass wall, Tyson taped up photos of the car seat, the pink baby blanket, photos of the tire tracks as well as the drops of denatured alcohol in the dirt. "The Boulder PD relinquished the evidence to our forensic expert. Russ and his team worked around the clock this weekend and confirmed the drops found away from the car were denatured alcohol. He hasn't matched the tire prints to a specific type yet. However, Russ did find two strands of hair clinging to the baby blanket, which have been identified as belonging to this woman." He taped up the Department of Motor Vehicles image from the driver's license of a long-haired platinum blonde with brown eyes. "Mia Turner. She was arrested and tried for arson ten years ago."

Nelson sucked in a breath. Had this woman torched the car? "Tried but not convicted?"

"Correct," Tyson said. "I've asked Jodie to work up a dossier on the woman. Nelson, you and Diesel go interview her. See if she has an alibi for Friday night's fire."

"Will do." If this woman was responsible for the burned car and the comatose woman, she might also know if there was a missing baby or not.

One way or another, Nelson would find the truth.

Sitting at her round dining room table, Mia Turner slammed down the phone and dropped her head into her hands. "Another cancellation."

The fourth today. Because of the negative online reviews.

Which she had no doubt were part of her business rival Ron Davies's smear campaign to put Jem's Rentals out of business.

Normally April marked the beginning of the seasonal equipment rentals and the hiking, kayak and canoe tours she led. But as of now, her calendar was blank. Which meant no money coming in to pay the bills.

Her great-uncle Jem, upon whose death Mia had inherited the business, had started Jem's Rentals thirty years ago. The company had been providing all the necessary gear for any activity on Dillon Reservoir, a freshwater lake in the middle of Summit County, Colorado.

Now Ron, a local that Mia had gone to high

school with, had returned to town from wherever he'd been for the past ten years and opened up his own equipment rental company near the marina. He was doing all he could to hurt the competition—namely her.

If this kept up, she had no idea how long she'd be able to keep the rental company going. It was her only source of income at the moment. Plus, she'd promised Jem she'd take care of the business that he was bequeathing to her. She wasn't going down without a fight.

She itched to give Ron a piece of her mind. Her fingers curled as she glanced out at the dark night visible through the windows of the cabin she'd also inherited. The two-story, A-frame structure sat among the spruce, pine and fir trees native to the high country. Her best memories were here at the cabin and the lake.

The bad online reviews and the tires slashed on Jem's old truck were mean-spirited attempts to drive Mia out.

The police had been no help when she'd filed a complaint, not that she expected assistance from them. She couldn't rely on anyone.

Her heart beat a bit too fast, and anxiety fluttered in her stomach. She took deep, calming breaths that did not work to ease the tingles of doom coursing through her veins. Why was she so edgy?

"Lord, please, give me peace," she prayed aloud.

Peace. A foreign concept.

Since the night of the warehouse party fire ten years ago, Mia had not known peace. She believed, with her whole heart, someone had planted the evidence that ruined her and her best friend Lindsey Gates's lives. There would be no peace until Mia exonerated Lindsey, who sat in jail convicted of a crime she hadn't committed.

A whisper of a noise outside the front window had Mia jumping to her feet.

Dread slithered up her spine, tensing her shoulder muscles.

Just the wind. Right?

Probably.

Maybe.

Or not.

The forest surrounding her cabin teemed with wildlife.

Or humans.

A blast of anger, born of frustration that someone—Ron Davies?—was trying to drive her out of business, and guilt for the seemingly good life she led while Lindsey sat behind bars, straightened her spine and lifted her chin.

She was done with being scared. She couldn't count on anyone else to protect her or help her. She had to take care of the situation herself.

She'd meet this threat head-on, whether human or animal.

She turned off the dining room light, throwing the cabin into darkness, save for the moonlight spilling through the windows. Silently, she made her way to the decorative storage cabinet in the kitchen, where she kept her weapon and all the research she'd gathered on the warehouse party fire.

Palming her Glock 9mm, she checked the chamber and the magazine. Not many people in Dillon were aware that she once held a PI license that afforded her the ability to carry and made her a good markswoman. She prayed she wouldn't need to use the weapon. But that would depend on whether she met with a predator or not.

She slipped out the back door. The moon shone bright overhead, the light filtering through the deep forest surrounding her home, and created shadows filled with unseen threats. Who was out here? Why were they tormenting her?

Because she was getting close to the truth of that long-ago night? Or was this simply more of her competitor's aggressive tactics to put her out of business?

Cautiously, she went down the back porch stairs and made her way toward the front of the cabin. A breeze off the lake sent shivers sliding over her flesh. The nocturnal sounds of insects and small animals foraging for food suddenly quieted, making her halt in her tracks. Unease raised the fine hairs at her nape.

An out-of-place sound, like a dog growling, had her turning her head to listen. She didn't have a dog, and as far as she knew, neither did her nearest neighbor.

A barrage of gunfire slammed into the side of the cabin, nearly taking her out. The noise was deafening. She dove to the ground, rolling until she bumped up against a stack of wood, providing her cover.

Someone was trying to kill her.

Gunfire!

Nelson crouched behind the large, older model pickup truck listing on flat tires and reeled in Diesel's leash, bringing the dog close. It took a moment for Nelson to realize the bullets were striking the other side of Mia Turner's cabin and were not directed at him.

Was Mia the target? Why? Did this have anything to do with the car fire? And most importantly, who was pulling the trigger?

A bubble of frustration lodged in his throat. It had taken him longer than expected to reach the high-country town of Dillon, Colorado. An accident on the highway outside of Denver had all lanes blocked for hours, making it past nightfall by the time he'd arrived at the address and parked a ways down the drive, wanting to get the lay of the land before approaching the house. The place was dark. At first, he had figured Mia wasn't home.

But then Diesel growled just as the first shots rang out.

A fresh volley of bullets pelted the wooden house. Answering gunfire from near the structure echoed through the forest.

Nelson withdrew his weapon and decided against turning on his flashlight. The last thing he wanted was to make him and Diesel a target. Staying crouched and in the shadows, he and the yellow Lab made their way around to the other side of the big truck. In the ambient light of the moon, he could make out stairs and a porch leading to the back door of the two-story cabin. Was Mia inside the house? Was she the second shooter?

The dossier report showed a handgun registered to Mia as well as an expired private investigator license. A surprising fact that had him wondering what the story was there. What had prompted a woman who'd been tried for a felony to become a private investigator?

The information he'd read on the warehouse fire and the charges brought as a result were straight forward. Mia and her friend, Lindsey

Gates, attended a rave party in an abandoned
warehouse on the outskirts of Dillon which ended
in an inferno that killed one person. Both Mia and
Lindsey had been charged with felony arson and
manslaughter. Witness accounts claimed Lindsey
had brought the accelerant to the party and Mia
brought the means to ignite it. However, Mia was
acquitted by a jury because the evidence against
her didn't support a conviction. Yes, she'd brought
a camp stove that ran on gel fuel to the party
along with popcorn, but the prosecution couldn't
tie her to the butane canisters that caused the
fire. Lindsey had been convicted and was currently serving time. The evidence against her—a
confession note found on her computer, multiple
cans of the accelerant found in the trunk of her
car and Lindsey's fingerprints on the remains of
the butane canister recovered at the scene—were
enough to convince a jury to render a guilty ver-
dict.

Despite what he read, Nelson still had questions. He needed to find out what was going on
here and now with Mia. But first, calling for
backup took priority. Using his cell phone, he dialed 911. After identifying himself in a low voice
to the dispatcher, he explained the situation. The
dispatcher promised to send a unit out right away.

Nelson hoped they arrived before anything
happened to his suspect. She was their only link

to the car fire and the coma victim. If Mia ended up dead, they had no leads to go on. No way to know if there was a missing baby or not. The stakes were high, and it was up to him to find Mia Turner and question her.

He contemplated putting Diesel back into the SUV, but he didn't want to take the time. His K-9 partner would protect him and sound an alarm, even though protection wasn't the dog's specialty. The mild-mannered Lab could be fierce when riled up. It just took a lot to rile him.

In a low crouch, keeping Diesel at his side, Nelson hurried past the porch stairs to the edge of the cabin. He peered around the side in time to see the muzzle flash coming from the forest as more bullets pierced the cabin wall but didn't hit the windows. Nelson couldn't see any specific target. Was the shooter's objective to scare, not kill?

Diesel gave a low growl.

"Diesel, quiet," Nelson whispered. He didn't want to draw the gunfire toward them.

Too late, Nelson realized Diesel was warning him of another threat.

The hard barrel of a gun pressed into Nelson's kidney. Diesel's growl deepened and he strained against the tight hold Nelson had on his leash.

"Don't move," a female voice whispered. "Who are you? Why are you trying to kill me?"

Nelson tucked in his chin. Surprise gave way

to chagrin at being caught unawares. "Miss Turner?"

The woman demanded again in a quiet tone, "Tell your cronies to stop shooting at me."

"Not my cronies," Nelson whispered back. "Miss Turner, I'm here to question you, not shoot you."

"Right."

Staying in a crouch, he shifted to face the woman. She remained in shadow, though he could make out her silhouette. Diesel stopped pulling at the leash and panted, obviously not seeing the gun.

"Put down your weapon," he said.

Ignoring his words, she asked, "If you're not with them, who are you?"

Before he could answer, another barrage of gunfire rent the air, this time the bullets definitely directed at them. Dirt spat up at him, inches away from where he huddled. The gunman must have moved so that Nelson, Diesel and the woman were in his line of sight. Nelson holstered his weapon and in a swift move, grabbed the gun in Mia's hand and wrested it away from her, effectively disarming her. She was after all a suspect in a crime that might involve the abduction of a baby.

She let out a yelp of protest. "Hey!"

Ignoring her outrage, he secured the weapon at his back in the band of his jeans.

More bullets whizzed past his head, splintering the wood of the cabin. He hooked an arm around the woman's shoulders and hooked his other arm around Diesel's neck, taking both the dog and woman to the ground, as he said to Diesel, "Belly."

The dog immediately dropped to lie flat in the dirt.

Nelson covered them with his body, wishing he'd put on a flak vest before leaving RMKU headquarters. He hadn't anticipated a shootout.

"Stay down," he commanded to both the woman and the dog.

He rolled to his side and unholstered his weapon. He aimed toward the last muzzle flash he'd seen and fired. A loud curse bounced off the trees. The sound of somebody crashing through the forest echoed in the stillness.

Mia pushed at Nelson and wiggled away until she was free. Jumping to her feet, she said, "I have to go after him."

Nelson grabbed her by the arm and yanked her back down. "Not in the dark, you don't."

A few seconds later, they heard the roar of an engine and a vehicle peel out over graveled rock. The shooter had escaped.

Mia yanked her arm away from him. "Who are you?"

Getting to his feet, he holstered his weapon and looped Diesel's leash around his hand. "Officer Nelson Rivers of the Rocky Mountain K-9 Unit out of Denver. Why don't we take this inside?"

He wanted a look at this woman, to see her face, her reaction when he asked her about the car fire. About the missing baby. And why a gunman was targeting her.

TWO

"You're law enforcement?"

Nelson didn't like that he couldn't see her expression. Not that he needed to; there was so much distrust embedded in her words that it was clear she had an issue with the police. Given her history, he wasn't surprised. "I am."

Grabbing his phone, he called the local dispatcher. He identified himself with his rank and badge number and then relayed what happened, not that he expected the suspect would be caught. Nelson had no idea what the perpetrator was driving or which direction he'd gone.

"How do I know you're for real?" she questioned as soon as he hung up.

Using his flashlight, he shined the light on his badge.

"That could be fake," she ground out.

"It's not." He turned off the light. "Look, if I'd wanted to hurt you, I would have."

Mia let out a huffy noise and marched past him

to the stairs. Nelson and Diesel followed her up to the porch. The screen door creaked open, and she disappeared inside, letting the door clang shut behind her.

Staying to the left of the door, just in case Mia had another weapon, Nelson eased the door open just as the lights in the house came on. He blinked against the sudden glow.

From deep within the house, Mia called, "Are you coming in or what?"

Keeping his weapon low at his side, he stepped around the corner of the doorframe and into the house. He heard a faucet running. Mia apparently had gone into the kitchen, giving him a moment to acclimate to his surroundings. No apparent baby paraphernalia in sight. He listened intently, filtering out the running water, but couldn't detect sounds of a baby crying or cooing. Was the child here?

The cabin's main living space was neat and tidy, if minimally decorated. He wasn't sure what he'd expected. More frills? From the dossier he knew she lived alone. A woman who was desperate for a baby might resort to kidnapping. Was Mia that sort of woman?

One wall had built-in bookcases filled with old leather-bound volumes as well as paperbacks. A plush chair sat off to the side of a worn leather couch that faced a TV in the corner. A blue-and-white blanket hung half off the couch. A coffee mug sat on the edge of the end table and a book lay on the floor in front of the couch.

He peered into the kitchen, again no signs of a baby.

Mia set a bowl of water on the floor. "For your dog."

Unusual thoughtfulness for a woman suspected of setting a car on fire and stealing an infant.

She stepped back, placing her hands on her hips, and giving him his first real look at her.

"You cut your hair." The words popped out of his mouth before he could control them. *Way to go, Rivers. You sound like a stalker.*

Her hair had been cut very short in a style he'd heard people refer to as a pixie cut. It matched her petite, slender form, making him think of Tinker Bell. He'd always liked the story of Peter Pan.

She wore jeans and an oversize sweatshirt that hid any hint of curves. The dossier he'd read before heading out said she owned an outdoor adventure rental company. She had the soft, sun-kissed glow of somebody who spent time outdoors. Her light brown eyes were framed by dark lashes, and she stared at him with wariness. She was pretty in a girl-next-door kind of way. But with her mouth set in a grim line, she looked anything but friendly.

"How do you know I cut my hair?"

"Your DMV photo," he said, regaining his composure.

She narrowed her gaze. "You don't look like an officer. I want to see your ID again."

He couldn't fault her thoroughness. He tugged the badge on the lanyard hanging around his neck from beneath his shirt and held it out for her to inspect more closely. Then removed his credentials from his back pocket and handed them over. "I'm legit."

He didn't wear a traditional uniform most of the time. None of the RMKU officers did. Civilian clothes let them operate with a bit more anonymity.

She studied the photo and information in the leather holder before handing both back. "Why are you here?"

He countered with, "Why was somebody shooting at you?"

Her gaze slid to the left before bouncing back to him. "I don't know."

He didn't believe her. Eventually she would tell him, but clearly, she was going to make him work for the truth. Which was fine with him. He'd always found it best to ease into an interrogation rather than go full throttle. He'd let her relax a bit and allow her to believe he wouldn't press for answers.

Instead, he switched gears. "Can I have your

permission to search the house to make sure the shooter isn't hiding inside?" And to see for himself if Mia had a baby stashed away. He'd have to get a warrant to search for the denatured alcohol used in the car fire. Unless of course she was careless enough to leave it out in plain view.

Her eyes widened. "Uh, I guess."

He made quick work of checking the rooms on the main and upper floors with Mia dogging his and Diesel's steps. Nelson found nothing to suggest Mia was hiding a stolen baby or fire accelerants. And Diesel didn't alert.

Back in the living room, he removed her handgun from his waistband. Though he knew the answer, he wanted to hear her story. "Do you have a license for this?"

Her chin tipped upward in a stubborn gesture that was both adorable and aggravating. "I do. A woman living alone, out here in the woods… I need protection."

Careful to keep any reaction from showing, he ejected the magazine and popped out the round from the chamber, then set the gun and ammo on the coffee table. "A 9mm Glock 43. An excellent weapon. Good for home protection."

Her eyebrows rose. "I'm glad you approve." Her tone said otherwise. "Why are you here, Officer Rivers?"

He purposely infused his tone with an affable

note. "I need to ask you questions about this past Friday night."

"Friday night?" Her expressive eyes showed confusion. "What happened?"

Watching her closely, he said, "A car was set on fire off West 84 near the Rocky Mountain State Park entrance."

Her eyebrows rose. "I don't know anything about it."

Keeping his voice even, he asked, "Where were you Friday night?"

"Here," came her clipped reply.

"Can anyone verify that?"

"What time?"

He'd received the call about the fire at 8:45 p.m. The wildlife fire management crew nearly had the flames out by the time he arrived. "Between seven thirty and eight."

Relief eased the tightness around her eyes. "Like I said, I was here. Alone. But you can check my landline. I had a phone call at seven that lasted for an hour."

"I will. Who were you talking to?"

She rolled her eyes. "I'll write his name down for you."

A man. Boyfriend? Accomplice? The one shooting at her?

She walked over to a console table behind the couch and took a piece of paper and a pen from a drawer. She wrote down a name and number, then walked over to him and jabbed it into his chest. "There, now you can go."

He caught her wrist, noting how delicate her bones seemed within his grasp. "Not so fast. Your DNA was found at the scene of the fire."

Her eyes widened and she jerked her hand away. "Not possible."

"Forensics don't lie," he said.

The stark anger in her gaze pierced through him. "Sometimes the forensics paint a picture that's not true."

He gave voice to the question her statement stirred. "Is that what happened to you ten years ago?"

She spun away from him, presenting her back. Her short hair brushed her nape, leaving the skin above her collar exposed. "That has nothing to do with whatever is going on now."

"But it might," he prompted. "I'll be the judge of that."

She spun and held up her hands, palms out. "I didn't set that fire. I don't know who did. I didn't do anything Friday night. Your forensics are wrong."

He had to trust the science. "We found two of your hairs at the scene."

"I wasn't there." Frustration echoed in each word. "It wasn't me. You have to believe me."

The words echoed in Nelson's head. He'd heard something similar once before, spoken just as passionately. He'd learned the hard way not to trust a claim of innocence, especially when there was concrete evidence to the contrary.

Forcing back the memory of his ex-fiancée's betrayal, Nelson tried for a different approach with Mia. "Do you know a woman named Kate Montgomery?"

He hoped Mia would shed some light on whatever had happened to put Kate in a coma, and on whether there was a baby missing or not. Did the shooting tonight connect to the car fire?

Mia's eyebrows dipped together. She shook her head. "The name doesn't ring a bell." She shrugged. "I have a lot of clients who come and go. I don't get all of their names. Only the ones who actually do the paperwork. And even then, I don't memorize them."

"So you're saying she could have been here?"

Mia let out a huff. "Maybe. I don't know. Who is she and what does she have to do with me?"

Good questions. "She would have had a baby with her."

"Then she definitely didn't rent from me. Infants aren't allowed on the equipment for safety and liability reasons. Sometimes one parent will come and hang out at the dock with a baby while the other takes their older children out in the canoes, kayaks or paddleboards. But that hasn't happened since last summer."

"Then why were two of your hairs found on a pink baby blanket at the scene of the fire Friday night?"

She stared at him for a long moment. "Were they long hairs?"

"They were."

"There you go." A measure of sass laced her words. "I have short hair, as you've already observed."

Not proof of anything. "You could have cut it today."

"I cut it six months ago, and I've kept it short." Then she made a little noise in the back of her throat. "I know. I donated my hair to a company that makes wigs."

He tucked in his chin. "You expect me to believe that story?"

"It's the truth." Her eyes widened with victory. "I have a receipt."

"I'll take that receipt. However, you could have grown your hair out and cut it after the car fire."

She rolled her eyes. "I didn't. I also have a receipt for my most recent visit to the hairdresser. Do you want that as well?"

"Yes."

Shaking her head with clear exasperation, she hurried into the kitchen and Diesel followed her.

Nelson frowned at the dog's wagging tail as he disappeared around the corner. When Mia returned, Diesel was right at her heels. The dog liked her because she'd given him water. That had to be why. The little traitor.

Mia handed Nelson the paperwork. He glanced at the receipt from the hairdresser dated two weeks ago. No way her hair could have grown as long as the strand found at the scene in that short amount of time.

The receipt from the wig company appeared legitimate. He noted it was dated six months ago as she'd claimed. She had donated eighteen inches of hair. Could the woman now lying in a coma have worn a wig made from Mia's hair? Was that why Mia's DNA had been found in the strands? He'd have to check with the fire investigators to see if they'd found any evidence of a wig in the car. There had been no mention of Kate Montgomery wearing a wig, though. For now, he'd accept Mia's explanation of how her hair had possibly come to be at the car fire, but if they proved otherwise, he wouldn't hesitate to arrest her.

Holding on to the piece of paper, he stared at Mia. "This doesn't tell me why someone was shooting at you tonight."

The sounds of sirens arriving snapped his attention to the backup he'd called. They'd taken their sweet time.

In the soft glow of the house lights, Mia blanched. "Great," she said. "This is all I need."

"You haven't answered my question," he said.

Heavy footsteps sounded on the porch, followed by a loud, jarring knock.

Without answering him, Mia marched past him to the door and yanked it open. Two Dillon police officers filled the doorway.

"Mia, what's going on?" the older officer asked. His badge plate read *Foster*.

She gestured toward Nelson. "He called you. You better talk to him."

Nelson frowned at her. Why wasn't she more upset that somebody had tried to kill her? What was going on here?

The officers stepped into the cabin. The younger officer hung back, while Officer Foster sized up Nelson. "What's this about a shooting?"

Nelson showed them his badge and introduced himself. "When I arrived Miss Turner was under attack."

The two men's eyebrows shot up. Officer Foster focused on Mia. "What did you do?"

"I didn't do anything." She moved to the couch and plopped down.

Nelson's jaw clenched. "Why would you think Miss Turner has done something to deserve being shot at?"

The two men glanced at each other without

explanation. They took their statements, writing down the details.

Officer Foster snapped shut his notepad. "We'll return in the morning and collect evidence. It's too dark out now."

Too dark? Seriously? They could use head-lamps and flashlights. Was their reluctance because of the discord he sensed between Mia and the local officers?

And they wanted to leave her alone and unpro-tected? "Somebody should stay here in case the shooter returns."

Officer Foster tucked his thumbs into his util-ity belt. "We're a small department. We don't have the manpower for protection detail. But you're free to call the chief and make a request. There's a lot of paperwork involved in something like that."

Nelson's gut churned. What if the shooter was out there just waiting for them all to leave so that he could come back and finish the job of killing Mia Turner?

It went against Nelson's nature to leave some-one unguarded if he could offer protection. "I'll stay."

The words jolted through Mia, and she jumped to her feet. "No, you will not."

She could not have this man, no matter how

different he seemed from the other officers taking up space in her home, stay in her house with her. She didn't need Officer Nelson Rivers. She didn't need anyone. She was fine on her own. She was a trained private investigator, proficient in self-defense, and a really good shot. If she hadn't come upon Nelson when she had, she was certain she would have been able to fire on the shooter again and hit her target. But she'd been sidelined by the man and his dog.

Officer Foster nodded his agreement to Nelson, as if she had no say in the matter. "Suit yourself, Officer Rivers." He looked at Mia, his gaze a mix of pity and suspicion. Something she'd grown used to from the locals ever since that horrible night. She was considered a social pariah. "We'll return in the morning, Mia."

She wanted to rail at him not to bother, but it would be futile and juvenile. There were times like this, faced with the distrust and hard opinions of those who were around ten years ago, she couldn't help but wonder if she should have left town when her parents had. But then again, the answers to what happened the night of the fire could only be found here in Dillon. And she wasn't going to rest until she discovered the truth. Could the shooting tonight be related to that long-ago fire?

Maybe.

Ron Davies. He seemed a likely suspect. Not only was he in competition with her rental company, but he'd also been at the warehouse fire.

The two officers left the cabin, closing the door behind them and leaving her alone with the canine officer and his dog. The yellow Lab lay down, resting his big head on his paws, his brown eyes watching her. It was both disconcerting and comforting.

Turning her focus away from the animal, she assessed the handsome officer. Why would he have offered to stay here? He didn't know her. She could only guess that he had some sort of superhero complex. He certainly was tall, muscular and had striking blue eyes that bore into her as if he could see into her heart. Maybe he'd glimpsed her hurt and heartbreak. She didn't need rescuing, she needed redemption, which he wouldn't be able to provide.

She crossed her arms over her chest. "You can't stay here." She pointed to the front door. "You need to leave. I can take care of myself."

"I'm not going to argue the point. We are staying." His tone held a determined note that made her wince. "We'll be out in our SUV."

"The temperature will get down into the low teens." Empathy squeezed her tight. She couldn't let him do that. "You can't stay the night out in your vehicle. It's not healthy for the dog."

She looked at the handsome Lab with his big brown eyes watching her. His tail thumped against the wooden floor, a rhythmic noise she found soothing. He really was a sweet-looking dog. She didn't have much experience with canines. Especially, working canines. Though she did love animals of all sorts. She couldn't subject the dog to such cold temperatures, yet she needed to make the officer go away.

Resigned to revealing part of her suspicions, she asked, "If I tell you who I think may be behind tonight's attack, will you leave?"

Nelson cocked his head. "I'm listening."

She gritted her teeth at the noncommittal answer. That was the best she was going to get from him. Clenching her fists, she said, "Ron Davies is most likely the culprit. The man is obnoxious and arrogant. I could see him pulling a stunt like this to scare me off."

"And who is Ron Davies?"

"My competitor." The burn of resentment sizzled through her. "He opened a rental equipment shop by the marina. He's been doing everything he can to try to put me out of business. He's posted negative online reviews, discounted his prices to nearly nothing. He's been giving away gifts to people who rent with him. I'm pretty sure he's the one who slashed the tires on the truck out front."

"Did you report this?"

She rolled her eyes. "Of course. A lot of good that did me."

"What does that mean? Why aren't the police taking you seriously?"

His intent gaze made her antsy.

"You know my history."

"You were seventeen," he said. "And acquitted. The local LEOs shouldn't be holding that against you now."

She pushed away the old, familiar ache spreading through her chest. "People in this town have long memories. And hold their grudges even longer."

Guilt and sorrow nearly choked her. She was doing everything she could to uncover the truth of that night, seeking redemption for both her and Lindsey. But she wouldn't share that with this man.

He was an officer of the law. Despite the assertion of innocent until proven guilty, that really wasn't the way the law worked. What had happened to her and Lindsey was proof. And despite how genuine Nelson's concern sounded, there was no way she could let down her guard. There was only one person she trusted. Xander Beckman had stood by her through the trial and the dark days after, when Lindsey had gone to jail.

But then Xander had left town, gone off to college.

Her parents had hightailed it out of town, too.

Only Jem had stayed by her side until his death.

But Xander was back now, preparing his family's property for sale because his parents had retired to Arizona. And he was her alibi for Friday night. He was the only one she could trust. The need to call him, to vent about the injustice of it all, rose sharply.

She headed to the front door. "There, I told you what I know. It's time you left." She opened the door.

Nelson shook his head, causing a lock of his brown hair to fall over his forehead. "Like I said, we're staying."

"But you said you'd leave if I told you what I knew."

One eyebrow cocked upward. "I said no such thing."

It was true he hadn't, but she had hoped he would be satisfied and leave once she told him. Frustration pounded at her temples, the beat reverberating against her skull. She just wanted him to go away so that she could be alone to process what had happened tonight.

But the man had a stubborn look in his bright blue eyes, which made her think he wasn't budging, no matter what she said.

THREE

Mia pushed the front door of her cabin closed with a sharp click. Acid churned in her gut. Her blood pounded in her ears. The lawman was staying, and the best course of action was to cooperate. Morning would come soon enough, and then he'd be on his way.

"Fine. I'll get a blanket and pillow for the couch." He would be uncomfortable on the too-short couch, but no way would she offer him Jem's bedroom. She looked to the dog and added softly, "And a blanket for Diesel." The dog shouldn't suffer.

Nelson's mouth tipped up at the corners. "We'd appreciate that."

She turned away, not liking how his smile affected her. She stalked down the hall to her linen closet, where she kept extra blankets and pillows. She consoled herself that she'd at least be upstairs away from the too-attractive officer and his cute dog.

But still, having someone in her home left her with a strange unease, not fear exactly, but more a cognizance of Nelson as a man. She hadn't had any company for more than a few hours at a time since Jem had died five years ago. She was used to being alone.

How would she sleep knowing there was a law enforcement officer and his dog just downstairs? The fact was, she wouldn't. She was in for a rough night.

Morning sunlight broke through the cracks in the curtains, stirring Mia awake. She blinked, her eyes adjusting to the light. The clock on the bedside table read 7 a.m. Her mouth dropped open. She'd slept a full eight hours.

Having expected to be awake most of the night because of her houseguests, she couldn't believe she'd not only slept well, but past the time she normally awoke.

It didn't make sense.

A bit off-kilter, she hurriedly dressed in jeans, a long-sleeve T-shirt in a light olive color and a pair of dark blue leather boat shoes. She darted into the bathroom to do what she could with her hair before she slipped downstairs.

Listening for noises, she heard nothing to indicate that Nelson and his dog were in the house.

The blankets were folded neatly on the end of the couch beside the pillow.

A strange disappointment invaded her. Puffing out an irritated breath, she pushed her displeasure away. Just because her psyche had relaxed and rested with the man and his dog standing guard it didn't mean she wanted to see the officer again.

He had to get back to his job and gave no consideration to saying goodbye. There was no reason for her to be hurt. She didn't need a goodbye. In fact, it was good riddance. She had a business to run and a reputation to repair. And an investigation to continue. She'd try to call Xander again as soon as she had some caffeine. He hadn't answered last night.

Stalking into the kitchen to make herself coffee, she caught movement outside through the sliding glass door and came to an abrupt halt.

Nelson stood at the edge of the woods near the path leading from the cabin down to the water and the rental shop. Diesel sat at his feet. Two Dillon police officers emerged from the woods. She recognized them as the same two who had shown up last night when Nelson had called for backup. One held a plastic evidence bag. She hadn't believed them when they said they would return in the morning to collect evidence. Apparently, knowing that Nelson would be expecting them had prompted the return visit.

The officers must have found shell casings. Maybe they'd find a fingerprint, and whoever shot at her last night might be identified.

Or if the perpetrator were smart, he would have worn gloves when loading the weapon. Was Ron Davies that smart?

If he had framed Lindsey for the warehouse fire, then, yes.

But why would he have framed Lindsey?

In Mia's recollection, Ron and Lindsey hadn't known each other beyond passing each other in the halls at school.

Still, the idea that Ron was involved lingered, if for no other reason than it was a new theory and she'd grasp at any straw she could find in her quest to exonerate her friend.

Ron had been at the party that night. Maybe he believed Mia got off unfairly. Now that he was back in town and had a competing business, he was trying to destroy her livelihood and run her out of town. To keep his own guilt at setting the fire from being revealed? Or was he just mean-spirited?

Too many possibilities. None of which she could voice without proof.

Nelson and the officers talked a moment before the officers walked around to the front of the house. Mia stepped to the archway of the living room to watch through the plate glass front window as the officers climbed into their white official Dillon police department vehicle and drove away.

Intending to find out what Nelson had learned, she headed back toward the sliding glass door in time to see him throw something down the path and the yellow Lab chase after, tail wagging. Diesel was all muscle and grace. He skidded to a halt to snag the toy and then loped back, looking pleased with himself. She smiled at the sight even as nervous energy raced along her limbs. The man and his dog were captivating.

Nelson turned, shielding his eyes against the morning sun, then waved, obviously seeing her through the glass.

On a breath, she stepped out the sliding door and stopped at the deck railing. "I'd thought you'd gone." She winced at the slight hint of accusation in her tone.

He tilted his head. "It would be rude to leave without saying anything."

Surprise and warmth spread through her chest at his consideration. "I saw the Dillon officers leave. Did they collect casings?"

Nelson nodded. "They did. And plucked bullets from the side of your cabin."

The spent bullets might also lead them to the shooter. Or at least to the type of weapon used, and if the bullets matched ballistics to any other crimes, might help the police with other cases. It was good to know they were taking the shooting seriously. All because of this man and his dog.

Suddenly not as eager to see him leave, she called to him, "Would you like coffee?"

"That would be great."

His smile packed a wallop. Disconcerted, she ducked back inside and started the electric water kettle. She glanced at the storage cabinet. Thankfully, the double doors were closed, concealing everything she'd collected in her investigation into the warehouse party fire. The last thing she needed was Nelson getting involved in her private business.

It was her responsibility to discover the truth. Her responsibility to exonerate her friend. She couldn't trust anyone else with the important task, despite how long she'd been trying and not getting anywhere. She wasn't giving up.

By the time she'd scooped the rich, ground espresso beans into the French press machine and poured hot water into the pot, Nelson and Diesel had come in through the sliding door she'd left open. Diesel went straight to the water bowl she'd left out for him. The sound of him gently lapping water as he drank was somehow comforting.

After pressing the ground coffee, she poured two cups and handed one to Nelson. He took the offered mug, his fingers brushing hers, creating tingles that raced up her arm. She quickly stepped back.

Tall and fit, he took up so much space. In the light of day, he was even more handsome. A night's growth of stubble darkened his strong jaw. His bright blue eyes seemed to take in everything, making her glad she'd run a comb through the short strands of her hair and brushed her teeth.

He sipped his coffee and made an approving noise in the back of his throat. "This is really good. What brand?"

Picking up her mug, she inhaled the rich aroma. "Illy. It's an Italian brand I buy online. The local grocery store doesn't carry it. My late great-uncle Jem was a fan. This was his house. He'd found the coffee brand on one of his many travels."

Curiosity shone in his gaze. "Have you traveled?"

"Me? Hardly. Not for lack of desire, but a lack of resources and time." She'd considered escaping all the judgment by going abroad many times, but there was no escaping the guilt over Lindsey's incarceration. "You?"

"A bit."

She waited for him to elaborate but he remained silent, drinking his coffee and watching her. Was he searching for fault? Guilt? She should be used to people assuming the worst of her. The idea of him doing so rankled in a way she didn't understand.

Unsettled by his perusal, she set her mug aside. "Is it okay if I pet your dog?"

Nelson's bright blue eyes lit up. "Yes. He's friendly."

She knelt down so that she was nose level with Diesel and tentatively put out a hand. Diesel sniffed her fingers, then moved closer as if giving her permission to stroke his head. He leaned against her, nearly toppling her over. She let out a laugh as she righted herself and slipped her arm around his neck for support.

"His coat's thick, almost hard to the touch."

"The top layer is definitely coarse, but the underlayer is softer and weather-resistant. He sheds a lot."

"I can see." She held up her hand with short yellow fur coating her palm. She stood, not sure what to do with the hair clinging to her.

"You can shake it off outside," Nelson said with a touch of humor tinging his words.

She stepped past him, so close his musky, masculine scent wrapped around her, setting her senses on alert. She hurried out the sliding door to shake off her hand and the strange attraction gripping her.

A nudge in the back of the knee drew her attention. Diesel had followed her out. In the kitchen, the sound of Nelson rinsing out his mug made her smile. Nice of him.

"He's shedding his winter coat," Nelson said, stepping out onto the deck. "I tend to vacuum a lot in spring."

"I've never had a dog." She crouched once again to pet Diesel. His tongue flicked out to lick her hand, the rough surface tickling her skin.

"He likes you," Nelson said.

Pleased, she glanced up at him. "How long have you had him?"

"We've been working together for three years," he said. "He was a year old when we started our training."

"I always figured police dogs were mostly shepherds with large teeth." She stroked Diesel's wide, well-shaped head. His breath fanned over her face and his nose twitched. Was he imprinting her scent into his memory?

"Different specialties require different breeds," he replied. "Diesel is an accelerant detection dog."

She stilled. Of course. She couldn't forget why Nelson and Diesel had come to her house in the first place. They'd arrived intent on learning if she'd set a car on fire, because strands of hair with her DNA had been found at the scene.

Anxiety twisted through her veins. She hoped he believed her about the wig. She'd given him the proof of her donation. There wasn't any more she could do in that regard.

Nelson had ended up chasing off a gunman. She was grateful and figured God had sent the officer and his dog when she'd needed them. But now it was time for Nelson to go. His presence wreaked havoc with her senses, not to mention he was in law enforcement, and she didn't trust anyone associated with the law. Not even a handsome, helpful officer with a lovable dog.

She rose and dusted her hands off on her jeans. "I'm sure you have places to be and criminals to arrest. I'll walk you to your vehicle."

"I'll stop by the police station on the way out of town and make sure the chief sends a patrol around to keep an eye on you," Nelson said.

"Please, don't do that." She hated the idea of any more attention being drawn to her. It was hard enough living in a town with the animosity from the past always surrounding her; she didn't want another reason for the residents of Dillon to be wary of her. "I can handle the situation. I don't need any more assistance."

His blue gaze never wavered. "Someone tried to kill you last night. They may come back and try again."

"I'll be fine," she insisted, praying it would be so. "I'll call for help if there's any hint of trouble."

He reached into the pocket of his jacket and

withdrew a small business card. Holding it out
to her, he said, "Here's my number."

Noting he hadn't said he wouldn't go to the police station, she took the card and tucked it into
her back pocket, doubting she'd ever call him for
help. There wasn't much she could say to keep
him from whatever he was going to do. Resignation was a familiar companion. "I really need to
get down to the rental office."

Not that she had any tours or reservations for
the day.

Ron Davies had seen to that.

It was past time she had a talk with Davies and
made sure he knew she wouldn't be intimidated
into going out of business. Not without a fight.

Nelson hadn't appreciated the way the Dillon
police chief had downplayed his concerns that
someone might try to harm Mia again. The man
had a giant chip on his shoulder where she was
concerned. Because of the fire from ten years
ago. The chief seemed inclined to believe Mia
had gotten away with the crime. But a jury had
acquitted her.

And yet the stigma lived on.

Keeping his reason for being at Mia's out of
the equation, Nelson had used his connection to
the FBI to ensure the chief had a patrol make
regular rounds at Mia's cabin and Jem's Rentals.

Telling the chief that her DNA had been found at the scene of a fire wouldn't have garnered any goodwill toward Mia.

Nelson had already contacted Russ Tate, the team's forensic tech, with the information regarding Mia's story about donating hair for a wig. The tech promised to check it out as well as search her landline phone to see if she'd made a call like she claimed. Nelson had called her friend, Xander Beckman, but the phone just rang before going to voice mail. He'd left a message asking the man to call him back as soon as possible. Nelson would try him again later.

Leaving the police station, Nelson drove to the marina area at the far side of the reservoir where Outdoor Adventures, the rental company owned by Ron Davies, was located.

If the chief wouldn't take action, then it was up to Nelson to make sure Davies understood he wouldn't get away with harming his competitor.

Nelson pulled into a parking spot and climbed out. He leashed up Diesel and then headed toward the rental office. The sound of raised voices, one he recognized, had him veering around the square building to the back where he found Mia and a large man arguing toe to toe. Mia barely reached the other man's shoulders, but she clearly wasn't in the least intimidated by the other man's size.

Nelson should have known she'd come here. She'd wanted to chase after the gunman last night, and no doubt considered it was a good idea to confront the man she'd decided was responsible for the shooting.

"I don't know what you're talking about," the man, presumably Ron Davies, said. He was big, bulky and had arrogance flowing off him. "You're making things up and I don't like it. That's slander."

"Talk about slander. You're the one posting false and damaging reviews online about my business," Mia countered, pointing her finger in his face. "You tried to kill me last night."

Ron held up his hands. "Whoa. No way, Mia." He glanced around and lowered his voice but not enough that Nelson didn't hear the warning in his tone. "You better leave or else."

Mia planted her hands on her hips. "No, you better leave me and my business alone or else!"

"Whatever." Ron made a dismissive gesture. "Go away." He smirked. "I've got clients to attend to. Can't say the same for you, huh?"

Mia's hands balled into fists as if she was about to take a swing at Davies.

Not wanting her to do anything she'd regret, Nelson and Diesel moved closer. "Mia?"

Her gaze jumped to his, her pale brown eyes widened, and her mouth pressed into a grim line.

Ron faced Nelson, flicked a glance at Diesel, then his gray eyes narrowed. "You're with the police?"

Logical conclusion considering Diesel wore his K-9 unit vest. Nelson showed Ron his badge. "Where were you last night?"

"Oh, man. You can't believe anything she says," Ron said. "She's a felon."

Mia sputtered a denial. "That's not true."

Anger tightened the muscles of Nelson's jaw. "Miss Turner wasn't convicted of a crime." Nelson took a step closer to Ron, crowding his space. "I asked you a question."

"And I'm declining to answer," Ron said, puffing out his chest. "You want to talk to me, contact my lawyer."

"I will," Nelson said. "Name?"

Ron reared back. "Seriously?" He groaned. "Mark Horton." He cast Mia a nasty look before turning on his heels and lumbering away.

"He did it," Mia said.

"Maybe. Maybe not." Nelson had a hard time picturing Ron being stealthy at anything. But as an officer and an army ranger, he'd dealt with enough suspects and insurgents to know first impressions could be deceiving. Ron Davies was a jerk, no question, but a would-be killer?

Nelson shifted his focus to Mia. "Why did you come here by yourself?"

She made a scoffing noise. "To tell him to back off."

Just as he'd suspected. "You need to be more careful."

"Look, I appreciate your concern," she ground out through clenched teeth. "But I can take care of myself."

As much as she might believe her words, Nelson had his doubts. If he hadn't shown up when he had last night...

Mia turned and walked toward a small compact car parked in the gravel parking lot near the walkway and climbed in. Nelson and Diesel followed. He caught the door before she could close it behind her. He leaned in to hold her gaze. "Listen, I'm worried for you."

Her brown eyes flashed surprise, then quickly clouded with wariness. "Thank you. But don't give me another thought. Really." She tugged on the door, forcing him to step back onto the curb so she could shut it.

He watched her drive away. A brooding sense of doom cloaked him. But short of putting her into protective custody, which he already knew she'd never agree to, he had no choice but to return to headquarters.

Diesel tugged at his leash, straining forward, his nails scraping at the loose rocks.

"What is it?" Nelson asked, letting out the lead

so the dog could get to whatever had him in a bother.

Diesel scrabbled forward and abruptly stopped to sniff something that had pooled, coating the gravel. Nelson bent down to examine what had Diesel so interested. As he touched the substance and rubbed it between his fingers, Nelson's stomach dropped.

Brake fluid from Mia's car.

FOUR

Mia gripped the steering wheel of the little sedan to keep her hands from shaking. So many emotions were rioting through her she couldn't hang on to one. How dare that creep Ron Davies threaten her!

It had taken every ounce of self-control she possessed not to reveal she suspected he might be the one who framed Lindsey, not that she had any evidence either way and accusing him before she could prove the allegation would only damage her efforts to absolve her friend.

And then Nelson and Diesel had showed up, witnessing her embarrassing display of temper. She couldn't get out of there fast enough. She owed Nelson an apology for snapping at him. But she'd been so humiliated by Ron and frustrated with the situation she hadn't been able to muster the words. Ron's business was booming while hers was languishing. It wasn't fair.

The red compact car in front of her suddenly

slowed to a halt, forcing her to step hard on the brakes. She caught a glimpse of a child's face in the back seat. For a moment there was tension in the pedal then it dropped to the floor, not decelerating the car at all. She pumped the brake. Nothing. She was going to rear-end the other car.

Panic bloomed in her chest. She cranked the wheel to the left, clipping the end of the car before her car shot across the oncoming lane. A horn honked. Tires screeched. The car slammed into the guardrail, and the sound of metal crunching against metal filled Mia's ears. The airbag deployed, smacking her in the face. Pain exploded behind her eyes and she slumped forward as the world faded to black.

Nelson drove along Dillon Dam Road, a straight stretch with guardrails on either side that circled the lake, toward Mia's cabin, hoping she was heading home. The cars in front of Nelson's SUV slowed, then came to a stop.

Dread gripped him in a tight vise. He sent up a prayer that the traffic jam didn't involve Mia. But the anxiousness in his gut warned that the leaking brake fluid Diesel had found where Mia's car had been parked had led to a dire situation. He needed to get to Mia.

"Please, don't let her be hurt," he said aloud.

It wasn't that he was emotionally invested in the woman, but the possibility of anyone suffering made his heart ache. He'd seen enough tragedies overseas in Afghanistan and while on the job to last him a lifetime. And if he could have prevented this one... Though he couldn't save everyone, he was still going to try.

Mia's image flashed through his mind, urging him to hurry.

He switched on his own vehicle's siren, pulled into the left lane and followed the ambulance until it halted at an angle, preventing Nelson from seeing what had happened up ahead. He cut the engine, giving the ambulance space, hurriedly jumped out and released Diesel.

Two Dillon police vehicles blocked both lanes of the two-lane road over the dam that kept the water from spilling into the lush little valley on the other side. A metal guardrail ran along both sides of the road. The biking and walking path on the lake side of the road created a barrier to the rocky shore of the reservoir.

As he and Diesel rounded the emergency vehicle, Mia's little blue four-door sedan came into view, and his heart stuttered. The front was crumbled into the guardrail, keeping the sedan from crossing the paved trail and hurtling into the lake beyond. A red two-door compact car with a dent in the back bumper was parked nearby.

Nelson's chest constricted. Was Mia hurt?

The driver's door stood open and two paramedics were tending to Mia, who appeared to be unconscious in the driver's seat. From the looks of it she'd hit the red car and then careened into the guardrail. The white, pillowy airbag lay limp in her lap. The medics put a C collar around her neck then carefully extracted her from the car and transferred her to a stretcher.

Nelson rushed to her side, pulling his badge on the lanyard out from beneath his shirt and letting it rest against his chest, where his heart beat in triple time. "How is she?"

Glancing at the badge, one of the paramedics said, "She has a head injury. We've got to get her to the hospital to determine any additional injuries."

She could have been killed. Impotent anger at whoever did this to her car roared through him. He searched the crowd on the walking path and those in their cars watching, wondering if the perpetrator was among those gawking.

"When you reach the hospital, notify security that she needs protection until the police arrive," Nelson told the paramedic.

"Is there something we should be aware of?" the paramedic asked.

"This was no accident." Though the only proof he had was his gut instinct.

The paramedic's eyes widened, and he gave a sharp nod. "Roger that."

They loaded Mia into the back bay of the ambulance. Diesel whined, clearly wanting to go with Mia. Nelson fought back the urge to climb into the back of the emergency vehicle, too.

"We will head over to the hospital soon," Nelson promised Diesel.

Some people considered talking to dogs as if they understood was a silly practice. But Nelson was confident Diesel understood.

Watching the ambulance make a U-turn then roll away, back the way they'd come, Nelson sent up another prayer of gratitude that Mia still lived and prayed the injuries were minor. Then he turned his focus on the officers who were slowly letting the traffic go by, one lane at a time. "What happened here?"

Glancing at Nelson's badge, the closest officer said, "Witnesses said the red car slowed but the blue car didn't. The driver lost control of her vehicle and smashed into the guardrail."

"Where's the chief?" Nelson asked.

"He doesn't come out for traffic accidents," the man said as he waved a silver pickup past the crash site.

Frustration bubbled within Nelson's chest. "When will the car be towed?"

"As soon as Harry's Towing can get here," the officer replied.

"Tell Harry's Towing not to touch the evidence," Nelson said.

"Excuse me?"

"You heard me," Nelson stated. "This is an FBI case."

"Oh, wow. Okay."

The officer looked impressed, which Nelson hoped meant the guy would do as he'd been asked. Nelson figured the small town of Dillon rarely had dealings with the FBI.

Nelson and Diesel hurried back to his SUV. He made a three-point turn and headed back toward Dillon's town center. Having already dealt with the police chief, Nelson knew the only way he'd get Mia the protection she needed was by seeing the chief in person. He arrived at the police station, leaving his SUV in a no-parking zone near the front door. He didn't plan to be here long. He leashed Diesel up and then hurried inside, straight for the chief's office.

"Hey," his receptionist said. "He's on the phone. You can't just go in there."

Ignoring her protests, Nelson pushed the door open and stepped into the office. The chief sat back in his chair, the phone cradled between his ear and shoulder while his hands wrestled a sandwich out of a wrapper. His eyebrows shot up. He sat forward, putting the sandwich down. "I'll call you back." He replaced the receiver. "Officer Rivers, I didn't expect to see you back so soon."

"Mia Turner just wrecked her car," Nelson told him. "It was not an accident. Her brake line had been tampered with and she'd been leaking brake fluid."

The chief steepled his fingers and placed his elbows on the desk. "What makes you think it wasn't just normal wear and tear?"

"After the shooting last night, it's an educated guess." Nelson couldn't keep the rage from vibrating in his tone. Was the man totally oblivious? Incompetent? Or did he really have such negative opinions of Mia that he just didn't care?

"I agree, that considering someone shot at her, her brakes going out could be construed as suspicious," the chief admitted, though skepticism laced his words.

"Beyond suspicious. She's on her way to the hospital. You need to put a guard on her," Nelson insisted.

"Now, see here." The chief stood. "You don't get to come in here giving orders. The hospital has security."

"You really want to face the scrutiny if something happens to her and you failed to provide adequate protection?"

The chief crossed his arms over his barrel chest. His eyes narrowed. "I can send one officer over."

"Good. I will make sure the hospital keeps her overnight for observation. I'll be back in the morning to take over." He and Diesel left the office and hurried out to the SUV.

He wasn't sure what his sergeant would think about Nelson and Diesel returning to Dillon. There was obviously something more going on here than a competitive business rival trying to put Mia out of business. There was something Mia wasn't telling him. He was going to get to the bottom of it.

Using his GPS, he found where the hospital was located and headed in that direction. He parked in the police designated spot outside the emergency room, then he and Diesel hustled inside.

"You can't bring a dog in here," the lady at the admin desk admonished.

Nelson held up his badge. "He's an officer. I'm looking for Mia Turner."

The woman frowned, checked her computer and pointed toward a set of double doors. "Through there."

With a sharp nod Nelson headed in the direction she'd indicated. He opened the door and held up his badge before anybody could protest. "Mia Turner?"

A nurse pointed to a curtained-off area. Nelson hesitated before opening the curtain. "What's her prognosis?"

The nurse, midfifties with short curly hair and kind eyes, said, "We're getting ready to take her in for a CT scan. We'll know after."

"Is she awake?"

"No."

He gave a sharp nod and then pushed the curtain aside to enter the small space. Mia lay motionless on the bed. The C collar had been removed from her neck. Her forehead was turning black and blue.

He didn't like seeing this spirited woman so still, so unresponsive. Diesel put his front paws on the bed and stretched upward, touching her hand with his nose. Nelson didn't blame the dog. In an incredibly short amount of time, Mia had endeared herself to them both. She was courageous, brave, and yet with a vulnerability about her that stirred him in ways he didn't like but couldn't deny.

However, involvement with his ex, Kelsey, had taught him that no matter how sweet or kind or caring a woman seemed on the surface, she could be harboring a dark secret. What dark secret did Mia Turner hold? And why was someone trying to kill her?

Mia was having an out-of-body experience. Floating. The sensation made her head spin. Then she was laid gently on a soft cloud. Was this what dying was like?

But she wasn't ready. She hadn't succeeded in proving Lindsey had been framed. She needed to exonerate her. Mia couldn't go to be with her Heavenly Father while so wracked with guilt.

The last thing she remembered was pumping the brakes and nothing happening. She'd tried hard to avoid hitting the car with the child in the back seat and managed only to clip the rear end as she'd steered her own car across traffic, aiming straight at the guardrail.

Something rough and warm swiped across her hand. This sensation was real, not cerebral at all. She forced her eyes open, wincing against the glare of the overhead lights.

"Here, let me turn those lights off." Nelson's voice wrapped around her, causing a riot of pleasure that was strange yet not entirely unwelcome.

Then the overhead lights winked out, leaving the room in a soft natural ambient glow from the high window. Even that amount of light stung, but at least she could keep her eyes open. She glanced around, noting the monitors, the bed rail, the exit sign. A hospital. In a private room. The last time she'd been to the hospital Jem had been dying from cancer.

Then her gaze swung over to her right and collided with Diesel's soft brown eyes. The constriction in her chest eased. He'd popped his paws on the bed beside her, his tongue lolling out to the side of his mouth. Was he smiling?

She must really be out of it if she believed the dog was happy to see her awake. But she couldn't deny how glad she was to see him. Then her gaze took in the man standing next to his partner. Nelson. For some reason his presence gave her comfort. For at least this moment, she was safe. He looked much the same as the last time she'd seen him, handsome and solid, alerting her that there hadn't been much time lapse between her accident and now.

"What happened?" Her voice cracked on the words.

"We can talk about that later," he said gently.

Her stomach dropped into the mattress. He didn't need to tell her. The brakes, or the lack thereof, had not been an accident. Another attempt on her life. She swallowed back the clawing fear. She tried to sit up. "I need to get out of here."

He gently pushed her back, his hands warm on her shoulders, the pressure somehow comforting. "No, you're staying put. They just did a CT scan. We're waiting for the results. But the hospital is going to keep you for the next twenty-four hours for observation. The blow you took from the airbag deploying was hard. Thankfully, it didn't break your nose but it did knock you unconscious."

Her insurance was going to love this. She hadn't met her deductible for the year. She didn't have the money for this stay in the hospital. Jem's Rentals hadn't been doing well for a while and barely made enough to keep the lights on. But admitting that to this man seemed like a defeat. "A bump to the head is nothing to be kept in the hospital for."

She also wouldn't admit to the pain behind her eyes or the throbbing through her brain. Or the ache across her midsection where the seat belt had dug into her flesh. She could be exploited for showing weakness, and she was never going to let anyone take advantage of her in any way. She'd trusted the police ten years ago to uncover the truth, but they hadn't. She could never forget that trust had to be earned. And this man might seem like someone she could trust, but letting her guard down would only cause her a different kind of pain.

"Always so independent and stubborn." A soft smile played at the corners of his mouth, highlighting his firm, well-shaped lips and drawing attention to his whiskered jaw, strong and bold. Just like the man.

She couldn't take exception to his words because they were true, but she was disconcerted that he'd made the observation. It somehow seemed too personal, too close to being known by him. A strange longing filled her, and she averted her gaze, not liking the attraction arcing through her. "Can I get some water?"

"Let me ask the nurse." He left her side.

But Diesel stayed.

She lifted her hand and placed it over one of his big paws. The dog did the most amazing thing: he put his other paw on top of her hand. Her heart squeezed tight, and tears sprang to her eyes. For the moment she could imagine this was what it was like to be cared for, deemed special. She didn't know why she was so emotional. Maybe because the police officer and his dog hadn't abandoned her?

Not liking where her ruminations were headed, she slipped her hand away from the dog. Unwilling to even allow that much connection. She'd learned long ago to stand on her own two feet without anyone's help. Relying on someone meant opening yourself up to heartache and pain. Betrayal and abandonment.

Nelson returned with a pitcher of water and a

small paper cup. He poured a cup of water, then set the pitcher on the rolling cart near the bed. He came to her side, slipping a warm, strong hand beneath her head and slowly lifted so she could take a drink.

"Easy now," he said. "Just a little. We wouldn't want you to throw it up."

Horrified at the idea of being sick with him standing there, she forced herself to only drink a couple sips, enough to wet her dry throat. Then he eased her back against the pillows.

She waited a moment as the world righted itself. "You don't have to stay here."

"I'm not," he said.

Unexpected disappointment spread through her limbs, making her eyelids heavy. The hurt was even more upsetting. Why should she be surprised? Everyone left her behind.

"There will be a guard outside your door for the next twenty-four hours," he said. "I'll be back tomorrow."

Her eyelids flew open. "You will?" She winced at the eager tone in her voice.

"I will."

The resolve in his voice held her enthralled. Definitely a superhero. Her hero. She almost laughed. She really must've smashed her head hard. No way could she let herself depend on him.

He gave her shoulder a squeeze. "I'm going to

check in with the doc before I leave. You need to rest. I want to see that feisty look in your eyes when I return."

She couldn't keep the smile off her face. He'd called her feisty. It was a lot better than some of the names other people had called her. "You better watch what you ask for," she quipped.

He gave her a lopsided grin. "There you go." His expression turned serious. "Please rest. Do not leave this room. If you need anything, you tell the nurse, she'll tell the officer, and the officer will call me."

His words struck fear deep into her heart. The man was really concerned.

Overly?

But then again, there had been attempts made on her life. She wasn't going to argue with him. She certainly wasn't going to admit how pleased she was to know that he was watching out for her or how much the attention and concern scared her.

Maybe it was that she was in a debilitated state, but she couldn't seem to build up the wall around her heart at the moment. All she could do was nod. "Thank you."

FIVE

After stopping at his house to shower, change clothes and pack supplies for both him and Diesel, Nelson went to the Rocky Mountain K-9 Unit headquarters, located in the same suburb outside of Denver. He headed straight for the sergeant's assistant's office.

Jodie Chen looked up from the paperwork she was reading. "Good afternoon, you two."

"Hi, Jodie, is the boss available?" Tyson's door was closed but Nelson could see him at his desk through the glass wall.

"Let me buzz him." She picked up the receiver on her desk phone and punched one of the buttons. After a moment, she said, "Nelson is here to see you. Can I send him in?" Tyson glanced at Nelson and gave a nod while saying something to Jodie. She hung up the phone and smiled at Nelson. "You can go in."

"Thank you." Nelson and Diesel entered his boss's office. Tyson's partner, Echo, a brindle-coated Dutch-shepherd mix specializing in drug detection, lay inside his open kennel and lifted his head at Nelson and Diesel's arrival.

Shifting to keep Diesel at his side, Nelson said, "Down."

Diesel sank to the hardwood floor.

Tyson's eyebrows hitched upward. "I was expecting you back from your task long before this."

"There was a bit more trouble." Nelson had filled Tyson in on the shooting last night and now related the events of the morning.

Tyson whistled through his teeth. "Someone has it out for this woman. Is it related to the car fire out by the national park?"

"Not that I can discern," Nelson told him. But he confessed what his gut was telling him. "There is something Mia's not telling me and whatever it is has put her life in danger. Someone shot at her and I'm positive messed with her brakes. I'd like to request permission to go back to Dillon and find out exactly what is threatening her life."

Tyson contemplated him for a moment. "I think that is the best course of action for the time being. If you find any correlation between what is happening to Miss Turner and the car fire, you let me know."

"I will. Any news on the driver of that car?"

"She is still in a coma. Does Miss Turner know our victim, Kate Montgomery?"

"Mia says no. Claims she has a lot of customers who come and go without ever getting their names. I was thinking I could have a picture of Miss Montgomery and show it to Mia. That might jog her memory."

Tyson nodded an agreement. "I take it then Miss Turner has no knowledge of the baby?"

"No. She's very particular about not letting infants on her rental equipment. I'm sure it's for insurance purposes."

"Rightly so." Tyson tapped a pencil against the desk, his obvious frustration coming through loud and clear. "I don't like the idea of a missing child out there."

Neither did Nelson, but there were still too many unanswered questions. "We don't know that one is missing."

"True." A grim light entered his eyes. "But I'd rather work off the assumption that there is one than dismiss the idea and be wrong."

Nelson agreed. "Did Russ tell you about Mia's donation of hair?"

"He did," Tyson said. "I don't get the science behind it. But he has been working diligently on the case. You might stop in and talk to him on your way back to Dillon."

"Good idea." Nelson would stop by the forensic tech's lab.

"Keep me in the loop." Tyson stood. "Make

sure you keep your phone on and charged. If we have any more fires, I want to be able to get a hold of you and Diesel." His gaze flicked to where the dog lay with his head on his paws. Diesel's ears perked up at his name.

"You can count on us."

"I know." The surety in his boss's voice pleased Nelson. Tyson had been a good leader on their many operations while deployed overseas and a great boss now.

Nelson's mind went to that last secret mission to rescue a high-level intelligence officer from an insurgent group holding him prisoner in a cave. They'd succeeded, but not without casualty. They'd lost a team member. There would always be a hole in all of their hearts where Dominick Young resided.

"Nelson, report to me what you find out about Miss Turner and who wants her dead. If she does have anything to do with the car fire and Kate Montgomery, we need to know. If you need assistance, don't hesitate to reach out."

"Yes, I will." Nelson and Diesel left RMKU headquarters and drove the couple miles to the FBI forensic lab.

The large lab space dedicated to the science of evidence collection and investigation was spotlessly clean with stainless steel tables hosting evidence containers. Lab equipment lined the walls—beakers, microscopes and vial containers were near at hand. A bank of computer monitors dominated another wall attached to a large internet server. Russ and his team were dressed from head to toe in white clean room garb.

Russ lifted the safety goggles from his face, the suction from the goggles' rubber seal leaving marks around his dark eyes. "What can I do for you, Nelson?"

Careful to stay back and away from any collected evidence for fear of contamination by either him or Diesel, Nelson said, "Tyson thought I should drop in to verify Mia Turner's claim of donating hair to a wig factory."

"Ah." Russ led them out of the lab and into a locker room where he stripped off the paper material covering his clothes and dark hair and peeled off the latex gloves. "Let's go to my office."

Nelson and Diesel followed him down a hall to a small office space with a desk piled high with file folders and other papers and books. A bookshelf crammed with volumes of science tomes looked like it might topple over from the weight.

Russ sat behind his desk and pushed some files out of the way so he could talk to Nelson. "Have a seat."

Nelson sat in the wingback chair offered. He

gave the hand signal for Diesel to lie down at his feet.

"Until recently, science has only been able to extract DNA from hair that has an attached root. Occasionally, the FBI manages to obtain a viable hair sample with a root for usable DNA."

"Did the strands you recovered from the blanket have the roots attached?"

Russ steepled his fingers. "No."

Nelson made a face. "Then how—"

Holding up a hand to stall his words, Russ said, "A scientific breakthrough. Until recently, a strand of hair without a root was useless."

The excitement in the forensic tech's voice was clear. Nelson leaned forward. "Okay. Go on."

"A researcher from California utilized a technique to extract DNA from fossilized bones and was able to create a genotype that allows for accurate extraction of DNA from rootless hair. To say this is a game changer is an understatement," Russ announced.

"Good to know." Nelson could only imagine the cold cases that could be solved with this type of science. Mia's words about science painting a false picture rang in his head. "You were able to extract DNA from the strands found on the baby blanket at the car fire and match them to Mia Turner."

"That is correct. I plugged the DNA profile into the national database and connected to her."

"Because the police had taken a sample of her DNA when she was arrested ten years ago." But in the car fire case, the science wove a narrative that put Mia at the scene of the crime. A false narrative, because she'd donated her hair for a wig. "And at some point someone wearing the wig had been in contact with the baby blanket?"

"That is a fair hypothesis."

Where was that wig? Who was wearing it? "Russ, I have a huge favor to ask."

Russ rubbed his chin. "Something to do with this case?"

"Not the car fire." Nelson had been given permission by his CO to look more into Mia Turner and to guard her. To do that he needed as much information as he could garner. "Though this does have to do with Mia Turner and a cold case from ten years ago."

"Are you referring to the warehouse party fire? Not a cold case," Russ countered. Obviously, he'd read Mia's file, as well. "Someone is doing time for that fire."

"True. But can you look into it for me?" He wasn't sure this would amount to anything than more work for Russ, yet Nelson's gut pushed him on.

"I'll see what I can find out," Russ said. "I can't

promise you how timely I'll be. I've so many cases running right now. The only reason I'm getting results quickly on the fire is Tyson expedited all the evidence."

Because there might be a baby missing.

"I understand." Nelson stood. "Text me with anything you find that might be relevant." He contemplated his request for a moment, then added, "Actually text me anything you find. I don't know what would be relevant and what wouldn't be at this point."

But he would, soon. Mia Turner was going to tell him what dark secret she was keeping. It was the only way to keep her safe.

"Is this really necessary?" Mia eyed the wheelchair the nurse had brought into her hospital room. The doctor had released her from care and now it was time to leave. She couldn't wait to be away from the beeping noises and the antiseptic smell that permeated the air and reminded her of Jem's last days.

She really needed to put on clean clothes. Her clothes reeked of the powder from the airbag. The nurse had helped her back into the outfit she'd had on when her car crashed into the guardrail.

"Yes, it is." The no-nonsense tone of the older woman shimmied over Mia, reminding her of Mrs. Hicks, her seventh grade teacher. Mrs.

Hicks had employed that same sort of tone to bring order to her classroom. Usually, Mia had been the one causing the ruckus. Mia and Lindsey. The dynamic duo. Her heart squeezed tight at the memory.

Nelson held out his hand. "Let's not give the nice nurse any grief. I'll help you."

He and Diesel had returned about an hour ago. Much to her surprise and, admittedly, relief.

As the morning had gone on, she'd despaired Nelson wouldn't return as he'd said. But he had and she was grateful. She drank in Nelson, who wore khakis, and a navy long-sleeve T-shirt that stretched across his broad shoulders perfectly. A jacket was folded over his arm. His bright blue eyes reflected the overhead lights, making them almost translucent. He'd shaved that strong jaw. Her fingers itched to test the smoothness of his skin. Floored by that wayward yearning, she could only blame the residual throbbing in her skull from the accident.

She'd had a fitful night's sleep, with the nurse coming in every few hours to check her vitals. She longed to get home, crawl into her own bed and pull the sheets over her head. Couldn't this whole nightmare go away?

That wouldn't happen, and wishful thinking was useless.

Thankfully, she wouldn't be going home alone.

Nelson and Diesel would be with her, and as much as she wanted to avoid relying on anyone, for now she had to. The dog hadn't left her side since he and his handler had stepped into her room. She admonished herself not to get used to this kind of treatment. Once they dropped her off, they would be leaving.

The jaded part of her whispered Nelson must have an angle. Why would he keep showing up like this? Offering help when he could just as easily go about his own business, forgetting she even existed?

He'd shown her a photo of the woman who'd been found at the scene of the car fire and was now comatose in a hospital. She hadn't recognized the pretty blonde. Did Nelson still think Mia had something to do with that car fire and the woman's injuries?

She hoped not. But she tended to be a worst-case-scenario thinker and had been proven right on more than one occasion. Like she'd known as soon as she and Lindsey arrived at the warehouse party that they didn't belong there. It wasn't a small get-together like she'd been told, but a rave, with loud music, drugs and alcohol. She should have insisted they turn around and leave. But she'd ignored her internal warning and stayed, promising Lindsey she would try to have a good time.

Nelson cleared his throat and raised his eyebrows, making her aware that she'd been lost in the past. She blew out a breath, hoping to calm the racing of her heart as she slipped her hand into his. Their palms met, his big and calloused, no doubt from the leash work he did with Diesel. She liked the way her smaller hand fit within his grasp. She liked the way warmth spread through her. He helped her from the hospital bed, holding her steady as she got her legs underneath her and the world rotated for just a moment.

Licking her lips, she met his gaze and realized in the shrewd way his eyes narrowed that he hadn't missed the moment of dizziness. She tried to stretch her lips into a smile, but she was sure it appeared more of a grimace. "I'm okay."

"Sure you are."

There was an undercurrent in his tone that made her bristle. He didn't believe her, nor should he. Even she realized her equilibrium was a mess at the moment. She got into the wheelchair, setting her feet onto the little flaps. And still Nelson held on. She glanced up at him. He smiled back. A genuine smile that made her heart do a funny little flip.

The nurse put a pile of paperwork into Mia's lap. "I'll push."

Thankful for the distraction, Mia broke eye contact with Nelson and faced forward as the chair moved toward the door. Squeezing through the doorway forced Nelson to release her hand. She gripped the edges of the paperwork. Diesel walked ahead of them at the end of his lead as they moved down the corridor toward the exit. His tail stood straight up and his ears were back.

Unease slithered crossed Mia's nape. "Why is he acting like that?"

At her side, Nelson's stride matched the rolling of the wheels of the wheelchair. "He knows he's on duty."

"Looking for fire?"

Nelson chuckled. "Always. But no, right now he's being protective. I've only ever seen him do that with my mom."

Pleased by the knowledge, Mia couldn't find fault with the man or the beast. As they went out into the morning sunshine, she blinked against the bright light and inhaled the fresh air. A new layer of snow dusted the ground and the trees. She shivered as the cool temperature seeped through her clothes. Nelson quickly laid his jacket over her like a blanket. She burrowed under it, liking the spicy and woodsy scent clinging to the material. Sandalwood. Her new favorite smell.

"I'll get my SUV." He handed her Diesel's leash. "Okay?"

Pleased to be trusted with his partner, she said, "Of course."

Nelson jogged away, leaving Diesel by her side. The big dog turned his brown eyes on her, his nose twitching.

"You have yourself a handsome protector," the nurse observed.

"Diesel's the best." She stroked the dog's head and scrubbed behind his ears.

The nurse laughed. "The dog, too."

Mia lifted her gaze as Nelson brought his SUV to a halt in front of her. She couldn't refute the nurse's words. Nelson was handsome, kind and considerate. But she couldn't forget he was also part of the system that had sent Lindsey to jail.

The awareness that she wasn't being fair to Nelson, or really others in his profession who had had nothing to do with the warehouse party fire, whispered in the back of her mind. She shook her head, hoping to dislodge the doubt.

Nelson jogged around the front of the vehicle and gently helped Mia into the passenger seat. His tender care made her heart ache. When was the last time anyone treated her so sweetly?

After securing Diesel in the back, Nelson climbed into the driver's seat. Once they were headed away from the Dillon Hospital, Mia sat back, finally letting herself come to grips with the fact that somebody wanted her dead and this man beside her and his dog were the only ones to prevent that from happening.

At least until she got better. She sat up and straightened her shoulders. She would get better. And once again be on her own. Carefully, she removed his jacket and laid it on the seat between them as if doing so was some sort of signal she was a strong woman who didn't need a man in her life. Because she didn't.

They made it to her house without incident. When Nelson came around to the passenger side of the SUV and moved to pick her up and carry her into the cabin, she swatted him away. "I've got two feet. I can walk."

His mouth twitched and he held out his arm. "Please tell me you won't rob me of the pleasure of at least helping you inside."

She wasn't sure who the gesture would bring more pleasure to, her or him. A pleasure she really shouldn't accept, let alone want. But as she took a step on wobbly legs, she grabbed his arm. Leaning into him, his sandalwood scent swirled around her, and she couldn't resist wishing that she'd let him carry her. What would it be like to be in his embrace?

Not something she was going to discover. Not if she wanted to keep her sanity and her heart intact.

Inside the cabin, he helped her to the couch. She sat down, sinking into the old leather and putting her feet up on the coffee table. Aches she hadn't noticed before made themselves known throughout her body.

"Are you hungry?" Nelson asked.

"Famished." The hospital had only fed her Jell-O for the past twenty-four hours. "I don't know what I have in the fridge." She hadn't gone shopping for several days. "There's bread and peanut butter."

"We can do better than that. I brought supplies." Nelson headed toward the door. "Let me grab stuff from my truck and then I'll make you some scrambled eggs."

"Wait. Your stuff?" He wasn't planning on sticking around, was he?

He turned to face her, bracing his feet apart. His gaze direct. "We're staying. You have a problem with that?"

Yes, she had a problem with that because she suddenly very much wanted him to stay. Which scared her nearly as badly as colliding with a guardrail.

SIX

Despite Mia's trepidation, she realized how ridiculous it would be for her to send him away until she recovered enough to not need him. She swallowed back the protest that rose to the tip of her tongue.

Taking a calming breath, which did little to alleviate the rapid pace of her pulse, she said, "No problem. That's fine."

Why did she suddenly sound like a squeaky mouse? She cleared her throat. "You can't sleep on the couch anymore, though." She wasn't that cruel. "You can use Jem's room." She pointed down the hallway.

He gave a sharp nod. Then walked out the door, Diesel trailing him. A shiver ran over her flesh, but it wasn't from fear or cold, but from something more primal that she really didn't want to acknowledge. She grabbed the blanket that Nelson had used the night before and pulled it over herself. She lifted the fabric up to her nose and breathed in his masculine scent that was out of place against the lavender fragrance of her laundry soap.

Mia had closed her eyes, letting herself drift. While he was around she might as well rest to speed her recovery. The slight screech of the screen door had her popping one eye open just to be sure it was Nelson.

He entered the house and she enjoyed watching him. Tall, muscled and handsome. He carried two bags of groceries in his arms, a big duffel bag slung over his right shoulder and another tote over the left shoulder.

Diesel came in and sat next to her, his eyes on her as if he had something he wanted her to know. She had to admit she was glad they were there.

After depositing the groceries in the kitchen, Nelson took his duffel bag and tote to Jem's old room on the first floor at the end of the hall. Once a week she aired out the room and washed the bedding. A habit she couldn't seem to break and one she was now thankful for because she didn't have to do a thing to get the room ready for a guest—it was stressful enough that Nelson was in her house.

When he returned, something compelled her to confess, "I should do something with all of Jem's stuff, but I haven't been able to bring myself to do it. Losing my great-uncle Jem was a hard blow."

Holding her gaze, Nelson said, "You will, when you're ready."

His understanding warmed her as did the way he looked at her with kind empathy.

He blinked and backed up a step. "Food."

He disappeared into the kitchen. The sound of him moving around was both disconcerting and reassuring. A few minutes later, he walked back into the living room and stood in front of her. The grim expression on his face had her stomach clenching.

"Care to tell me what's going on inside the storage cabinet?"

She clenched her jaw to keep a groan from escaping. She hadn't closed the double doors on the piece of furniture that housed the collection of information she'd gathered when she'd left the cabin earlier. Which allowed him to see the results of her investigation. There was no way he was going to let that go. "I'm doing my own investigating into the warehouse party fire."

Nelson had already guessed she was investigating the warehouse fire because she had the crime scene photos, police and fire investigation reports hidden away in the storage cabinet. However, having her confirm his supposition filled him with a strange sense of dread.

Was this why she was being targeted? "For how long?"

She sat up, lifting her chin. "Three years."

Three years of putting herself in danger. "You should leave the investigation to professionals."

"Professionals?" she scoffed, though there wasn't a lot of heat behind the sound. "I am a professional. I have a PI license. I know what I'm doing."

Amateurs playing sleuth didn't always end well. An expired private investigator's license hardly qualified her to be delving into a closed police case. "Why?"

She scrunched up her nose. "Why what?"

Holding on to his patience, he said, "Why do you have a PI license?"

"After the trial—" She looked away.

He could see the delicate way her throat worked as if she had to dredge the words from deep within her. He waited, letting her find her voice.

Finally, she continued, stronger, determined. "My parents couldn't take the notoriety or the shame of their only daughter being accused and tried for a crime. The whole town made it hard on them. On me. On Lindsey. No one believed our claims of innocence."

Sorrow for what she must have gone through constricted his chest.

"Great-uncle Jem let me live with him. I'd spent most summers, holidays and weekends working for Jem's Rentals rather than in my parents' restaurant." She gave a dry mirthless laugh. "Another way I'd disappointed my parents."

The pain in her tone had him moving to the end of the couch. He sat and remained quiet.

She glanced at him, her pale brown eyes shiny. "I hated the helplessness of watching my friend go to prison, but what could I do? Lindsey's parents were indifferent. My parents basically disowned me. I barely managed to finish high school. It was torture going to classes every day."

Though Nelson hurt for her, he reminded himself he needed to stay detached. Unemotionally involved. This woman garnered his sympathies but was she telling the truth? Should he believe that she really wasn't complicit in the fire even though she was acquitted?

She blew out a breath. "Then Jem suggested I look into taking some college classes. At first I didn't see the point, but once I started I found my purpose. I graduated with an associate degree in criminal justice from Colorado Mountain College. It took me longer than the normal two years because I had to work to put myself through school."

"Good for you." He had to admire her grit and

determination. It must have been difficult staying close to Dillon and attending college.

She shrugged. "I went through the process of gaining my private investigator license, which took several years as I did my practicum hours with a PI friend of Jem's in Denver while working in a restaurant to make ends meet. I moved back here when Jem got his diagnosis."

"That's when you started looking into the warehouse party fire? Can you tell me more?" Though he'd read the details of the event, there was nothing like hearing a personal account to fill in blanks. Dry reports couldn't reveal emotions which often lent themselves to motive. Not to mention sometimes the story changed. Lies were hard to keep straight.

"Neither Lindsey nor I started that fire," she insisted with passion lacing each word. "I owe it to my friend to figure out what really happened." She sliced the air with a hand. "If I hadn't talked her into going to that party… If I had gotten us out of there when I realized what it was turning into… If I hadn't stepped away from the camp stove—"

"That's a lot of ifs. And a lot of guilt to carry."

"I would have been able to see the danger of an open butane canister near the flame and would have done something about it," she argued. "I was the one familiar with the equipment, not Lindsey.

But neither of us brought butane. I don't know where it came from."

"Why are you the one who has to find the answers?"

She closed her eyes. "I have no choice. I have to exonerate Lindsey. She was there that night because of me."

"You don't trust the court system," he stated, knowing full well she didn't and why. If the way the local police treated her was any indication, she had reason.

She stared at him. "No. The police came up with one conclusion and wouldn't look for any other explanation. And the prosecution did everything in their power to make us look guilty."

"But the evidence—"

"Was planted," she interjected.

This was unexpected. He would need to reread the police report. "Planted?"

"Yes," she insisted. "Someone framed us. Framed Lindsey."

He tucked in his chin as he digested her claim. From what he could remember of the file, the investigators had had no hint of doubt. "They found butane canisters in the back of Lindsey's car. And the confession note on her computer. Plus, there were witnesses who said they saw her with a canister at the party."

She scoffed. "Anyone could have planted those

cans. Someone hacked her computer and wrote the note." She sighed heavily. "She didn't have a canister at the party. I was with her the whole time. Well, not the whole time. I let someone talk me into dancing."

"There's no crime in that," he murmured. If what she said was true, she had no way of knowing what would happen. "In the police report Lindsey stepped outside at some point."

"Yes. Because she was nauseous." Her eyes pleaded with him. "We didn't bring those canisters. The camp stove ran off a gel fuel. I would never bring compressed gas. It's too volatile. I thought making popcorn would be fun. It was only supposed to be a few of us from our math class meeting at the warehouse. But apparently, the news of the gathering swept through the high school and everyone turned up. Along with drugs and alcohol."

He resisted the desire to believe her. He'd made that mistake once before with a woman whom he'd believed he'd known. Whom he'd trusted. Loved even. Only to find out she was a liar and a cheat. "I assume you said all this to the police, and they didn't believe you." Which would explain the chief's attitude.

"They didn't believe us. And because we arrived together and were friends, the prosecution charged me as a co-conspirator. We didn't do this. Seaver was killed, and the town was out for blood. Our blood."

Seaver Johnson, the son of the mayor at the time, Nelson recalled reading in the file. The boy had died, and someone had to pay.

Sadness filled her pale brown eyes. "I don't know what he was doing there. It wasn't his kind of scene. Seaver was the brightest kid in school. A gifted piano player. And asthmatic. He inhaled smoke and perished before help arrived."

Empathy twisted in Nelson's chest. A horrible way to die.

"It was Xander who carried Seaver out, but it was too late."

His eyebrows shot up. "Xander? The same guy who is your phone call alibi for last Friday night?"

"Yes. He's the only one who stuck by me during the trial and the dark days afterward. Until he left for college. Now he's a successful businessman. He returned because his parents wanted to sell their home and acreage."

He filed that information away. He still hadn't been able to verify Mia's claim that she'd been talking to Xander. Russ had confirmed her landline had been in use at the time; however, the phone had been connected to a burner. "Have you learned anything useful?"

"I don't know. There's still so much I need to

uncover and people I need to question, but many won't talk to me and others I can't find."

Her frustration was tangible. "Assuming you're right that someone tried to frame you and Lindsey—" he wasn't sure he bought that notion "—who would do it? And why?"

"Those are the million-dollar questions, aren't they?"

She sounded so weary and deflated that he decided to table the discussion. He needed time to process what she'd told him, and she needed food plus rest. Tomorrow he would dig into her investigation and put a stop to it. "We can talk more about this in the morning." He rose. "I'll bring you a plate."

"Thanks." She gave him a wan smile.

He fed Diesel, then made scrambled eggs and toast and brought their plates into the living room. She'd turned on the television to the news report. As the weatherman gave the forecast for the week, they ate. Diesel lay on the ground near his feet.

Setting her plate aside, she said, "Scrambled eggs never tasted so delicious."

"I figured something mild would be a good choice." He picked up their plates as the news flashed "special alert" across the screen.

"Just in," the newscaster said. "The authorities are looking for any information regarding missing hiker Emery Rodgers." A picture came onto the screen of a blonde, blue-eyed woman. "Emery was last seen in the parking lot of the Santa Fe Ski Basin in the Southern Rockies. If you have any information, please contact authorities."

Nelson wondered if members of the K-9 unit would be called to the scene to help in the search.

"She probably went off the trail and got lost or hurt," Mia said. "I've hiked that basin. It's wooded and steep."

"I pray they find her soon," he said. "Unharmed."

"Me, too."

They shared a smile. For some reason, knowing she had faith warmed his heart. But then again, he'd assumed his ex-fiancée had shared his faith and fidelity.

He turned away to take their dishes back to the kitchen but halted when the newscaster said, "In other news, the trial for William 'the Hawk' Hawkins, the man accused of killing Congresswoman Natasha Clark, is set to begin next month." The reporter went on to relate the details of the murder of one of the state's sitting members of congress.

"That's scary," Mia said. "Wouldn't she have had protection?"

"One would think so."

After putting their dishes in the dishwasher and

tidying up the kitchen, he found Mia stretched out asleep on the couch and Diesel lying on the floor in front of the couch. Not wanting to disturb Mia, Nelson adjusted the blanket fully over her, then slipped off her shoes, setting them under the coffee table. Diesel lifted his head for a moment to watch.

Marveling how the dog had already attached himself to Mia, Nelson bent to remove his collar. Diesel had never liked Nelson's ex-fiancée. Nelson should have taken that as a sign. He straightened as that realization rocketed through him. Did Diesel's approval of Mia mean Nelson should believe her? Believe in her?

He recoiled from the idea. He wasn't going to let his guard down. Not until he was sure. Just what he was waiting to be sure of, he couldn't say. Nor what outcome he expected.

Pushing away that line of thinking, he checked the doors and windows, satisfied that the cabin was locked up tight before he headed to the bedroom on the first floor. He changed into black sweats and a long-sleeve thermal shirt. Grabbing the blankets off the bed, he returned to the living room. He put another blanket over Mia, then settled in the overstuffed chair in the corner with a blanket. He wanted to be close by. He wasn't going to let any more harm come to her.

* * *

Hours later, Mia blinked awake to find Nelson asleep in the corner chair and Diesel lying by the front door. The sun was low in the sky and filled the cabin with a warm glow, despite the chill in the air from last night's dusting of snow.

Careful not to make any noise to wake Nelson, she slipped from the couch and padded in her socks across the rug covering the cabin's hardwood floors to the stairs. She had a slight headache and her body was sore, but overall, she was in good shape.

Upstairs, she cleaned up, glad to have the hot water wash away the grime of the accident. The bruise on her face where the airbag connected was ghastly, as was the bruise across her chest, but both would heal. In her bedroom, she changed into a fresh set of jeans and a lightweight sweater. Before heading back downstairs, she paused to touch the photo she had of Jem on her dresser by the window. She missed her great-uncle.

Her gaze strayed out the window to the equipment rental building visible through the trees. Little more than a shed that housed the gear and apparatus that Uncle Jem had collected over the years, the structure had a roll-up door in the rear, and a door in the front flanked by windows. A long dock protruded from the shore into the water with a couple of kayaks and canoes moored to the sides. So many memories were tied up in working inside the shop and out on the lake.

How was she going to make the business a success with Ron Davies driving away her customers? Was he also trying to kill her? If so, did he simply want to put her out of business or was his intent to keep her from finding out the truth of the fire? He was one of many who were at the warehouse party that night. And she remembered Ron had been a hot head in high school. He'd been on the football team and considered himself a big man on campus. But did that make him an arsonist? A would-be killer?

She blew out a breath to release some of her frustration. Movement in the rental shop window caught her attention. Had an animal somehow gotten inside? Just what she needed, a raccoon or deer eating the life vests. Or it could be worse—the killer was there waiting for her to open up.

She rushed downstairs to tell Nelson.

Nelson, looking adorable with his messy hair and sleepy eyes, sat up in the chair as she entered the living room.

For a second all she could do was stare. He was really such a gorgeous man in so many ways. Good-looking but considerate and kind, too. She blinked away the attraction to say, "I think an animal got into the rental shed. At least, I hope it's only a four-legged beast."

Concern flashed in his eyes and he vaulted to his feet. "We'll go check it out."

"Not without me." Spying her shoes under the coffee table, she reached for them, her heart stuttering. Nelson must have removed her shoes from her feet last night after she'd fallen asleep. She sat on the couch to put them on.

Anxious to chase away whatever critter had found its way inside the rental shed, and praying it wasn't of the human variety, she headed to the back door. As soon as she opened the slider, Diesel bolted out of the cabin for the grass.

Nelson stepped out a second later with a leash in his hand and his feet jammed into a pair of running shoes. He gave a whistle, and the dog trotted to him, allowing him to attach his lead. Then the three of them walked down the dirt path through the trees to the rental shed.

As they neared the structure, Diesel emitted a low growl.

A loud crash from inside the shed jolted Mia's heart into overdrive.

Nelson held up a hand, halting them in their tracks. In a low voice, he said, "Stay behind me."

He lifted his shirt enough to reveal the holster attached to his sweatpants and removed his weapon. He and Diesel approached the shed from the front. Nelson pressed his back against the wall near the door.

Mia circled around to the back, noting a beached aluminum fishing speed motorboat near the dock she hadn't seen from the window. Unease prickled her skin and twisted in her gut. Could the animal inside the shed be of the two-legged variety? She had to warn Nelson. She ran around the structure in time to hear Nelson shout, "Stop, police."

Diesel's ferocious barking pierced the air. Nelson and a big man dressed in black with a balaclava covering his face wrestled for possession of Nelson's gun. Diesel snapped at the assailant and grabbed a hold of the man's pant leg, dug his paws into the ground and pulled at the attacker.

Heart-pounding anger swept through Mia. She reached inside the open door of the shed for a kayak paddle and came out swinging at the intruder. The paddle landed a good hit on the man's shoulder. He yowled and released his hold on Nelson and gave a forceful shove that made Nelson fall hard on his back.

Mia swung the kayak paddle again, but the attacker dodged the blow, shook off Diesel, leaving the dog with a mouthful of fabric, and ran past the building out of sight toward the lake and the boat.

SEVEN

Nelson scrambled to his feet and chased after the assailant. Mia stayed on his heels, unwilling to let him defend her property alone.

The attacker jumped into the fishing boat, fired up the motor and sped away across the lake and disappeared around the bend.

Diesel dashed to the water's edge. A sharp whistle from Nelson brought the dog trotting back, but then the yellow Lab stopped, lifted his nose in the air and swiveled toward the dock just as a slight popping sound echoed over the lake and the dock burst into flames. The sight sent a jolt of horror racing through Mia.

"Diesel, come," Nelson shouted. The dog ran to him.

Mia's heart sank.

Fire licked at the wooden platform. The canoes and kayaks her business depended on were in grave jeopardy from the growing flames eating at the shore-side end of the dock.

"Oh no. Please, Lord," she said aloud, though deep inside she wasn't sure He would listen to her. He'd been silent for so much of her adult life.

She and Nelson raced to the water's edge and waded past the burning dock to collect the canoes and kayaks moored to the sides of the wooden dock and drag them ashore. Heat from the encroaching flames blasted against her, making her wince. She splashed water on the flames, but her efforts met with little success.

Wanting desperately to save as much of the dock as she could, she slogged her way out of the water. "The hose!"

Nelson nodded and followed in a rush to the cement platform that housed the powerful hose she used to wash the rental equipment. She turned on the spigot, while Nelson dragged the hose as close to the burning dock as he could get.

The treated wood burned incredibly hot and filled the air with billows of dark, choking toxic smoke that stung her eyes and lungs.

She pulled her shirt up over her nose and mouth as she joined Nelson, grabbing the hose and cranking the hose valve open to release a spray of water. Together, they fought back the flames. Tears streaked down her face. A scream of anger filled her chest.

Sirens split the air. Surprise and gratitude that someone had called 911 had her sobbing as they continued to douse the flames. She sent up a prayer of praise. She could only guess that some-one on the lake had seen the smoke.

The Dillon Fire Department arrived, pulling into the small parking lot off to the side of the rental shed. Firefighters added their hoses to hers. Soon the end of the dock was a soggy mess.

She sagged in relief and closed the valve on the hose she held. Nelson took it from her shaky hands.

The fire chief, Stan Clemens, moved to stand beside them. He'd been one of her dad's friends and a patron of her family's restaurant before her parents had closed down and moved away. "Mia, care to tell me what happened here?"

"A guy in a fishing boat set the dock on fire." She forced herself to remain calm.

Nelson revealed his badge and proceeded to tell the fire chief about the intruder.

"The police are on their way," Stan said.

As the fire crew worked, Mia used the end of the kayak paddle to scoop up the ripped piece of the assailant's pant leg Diesel had spat out. "I've got a bag in the cabin for this."

Nelson nodded. "Good. Not sure it will be use-ful, but I'll send it to the FBI's evidence expert."

Planting the paddle in the ground with the evi-dence draped over the top, Mia stepped into the shed. The intruder had ripped up the life vests, toppled over the stacks of equipment, and used a hammer to pound holes in the canoes and kayaks that hadn't been moored to the dock. On the interior of the roll-up door the word *FELON* had been spray-painted in red.

"Ron Davies used the word *felon*," she muttered, remembering the sneer in Ron's voice when she'd confronted him at his rental shop.

"That he did." Nelson stood beside her. "I'll help you clean this up after the police are done with the scene."

"I doubt they will find anything. The guy had gloves on." She couldn't keep the frustration from her voice. Her headache intensified. "It was Ron Davies. He's the one trying to hurt me."

"Why are you so sure?"

She debated voicing her suspicion. Would he believe her? Or dismiss her theory with a mocking smirk the way law enforcement had since the day she started questioning the investigation into the fire? The chief of police and the county prosecutor both considered the matter closed. Even Xander believed she was "spinning her wheels," as he put it. No one wanted to contemplate a scenario that included someone other than Lindsey starting that fire.

A Dillon police cruiser drove up, stalling her answer. She stood back and let Nelson deal with the two officers. They took their statements and promised to look into anyone with a silver fishing boat that might have been on the lake in the past hour. Mia wasn't going to hold her breath.

"You didn't give them the piece of evidence," she commented as they watched the cruiser drive out of the small parking lot. The fire crew departed as well.

"The FBI lab will have more success and be quicker." He picked up the paddle, keeping the black material carefully balanced over the end.

She stared at him for a moment, marveling that he was willing to help her. Of course, he'd fought with the attacker and no doubt wanted to bring the man to justice for that reason only. But still, she liked the idea of having someone on her side.

Before she could talk herself out of it, she said, "Let's go back to the cabin and clean up. Then I'll show you my investigation."

Inside the cabin, Mia offered Nelson a brown paper bag for the piece of fabric. He wrote on the outside the date and time.

The reminder of the intruder at the shed made her shiver. Things could have gone very badly. Nelson could have been shot. If he hadn't been here and she'd gone to the shed alone, who knows what would have happened to her. They'd saved each other. The knowledge was both comforting and distressing. Next time might not end as well.

Diesel drank from the bowl of water, nearly

depleting it all. After refilling the bowl and setting it back down, she hurried upstairs to change into dry clothes.

When she returned, Nelson had also freshened up and now wore faded blue jeans and a pullover sweatshirt. Tearing her gaze from him, she faced the storage cabinet and opened the doors wide. Awareness of Nelson watching her closely shimmied up her spine and settled like hot coals in her cheeks.

She was tempted to slam the doors shut and tell him it was none of his business, but a part of her wanted to trust him. She'd been going it alone for so long, the concept of having someone else to help shoulder the burden appealed to her on so many levels. Still, she hesitated. Would he find fault with her attempts at exonerating Lindsey?

"Walk me through your investigation," he said.

Diesel moved to sit at her feet as she proceeded to show Nelson the case files and photos from the fire. Having the dog lean on her somehow bolstered her courage to reveal all she had been doing for the past three years.

"The arson investigation reported the fire started when the camp stove had come into close contact with an open butane canister that blew up, sending flames to ignite the wooden pallet the camp stove sat on and the wooden walls of the building." The pallet she'd set the camp stove on. At the time it seemed a good spot to cook from but now she regretted that night with every fiber of her being. Anxiety withered inside her gut. There hadn't been any canisters of butane around. She was sure of it.

Though he'd no doubt already read the case file and knew the details of the fire. But what wasn't in the case file were the echoes of the terrified screams or the acrid taste of smoke. The horrible images still haunted her nightmares. "On one piece of metal recovered at the scene, determined to be from the butane canister that had ignited, was a set of fingerprints. Lindsey's."

The admission carved a groove through her. Nelson's unreadable expression made Mia's heart pound. Diesel nudged her with his nose. Because of her short stature, she didn't have to bend at all to reach out and stroke a hand over his head. The contact grounded her. Soothed her. Allowed her to speak about the worst moment in her life. "The prosecution theorized I had brought the camp stove and Lindsey had brought the butane. And together we conspired to set the warehouse on fire."

She watched him closely. Would she see judgment? Condemnation?

He crossed his arms over his chest, his face remaining frustratingly impassive. "The motive?"

Nelson's soft question stirred old anger. Her

hands fisted at her sides. Again Diesel's wet nose touched the back of her hand as if to offer comfort. "We had no motive. Because we didn't do it. The prosecutor claimed we were outcasts and wanted to punish the cool kids."

"Were you outcasts?"

She shrugged, old hurts scratching at her. "Not exactly. Lindsey came from a bad home. Her father drank and her mother was like a shadow, barely leaving the house, which left Lindsey to her own devices. She got into trouble a lot. My parents, on the other hand, were strict and very regimented." She forced back the anguish of talking about this. She needed to stay detached, unemotional. Keep the facts at arm's length out of habit, to protect herself from more hurt and torment. "Our family's restaurant did a good business and took all their focus. They expected me to devote the same attention to their dream. But I hated being cooped up inside all the time."

Her hand strayed to Diesel's broad, silky head again. "I guess I had my own streak of rebellion. I'd sneak away and goof off at the lake or hide here at Jem's until my parents finally gave up and granted me permission to hang here. Lindsey and I gravitated to each other in grade school. And gravitated to trouble." She dropped her gaze to the dog's nonjudging, big brown eyes and swallowed away the guilt. "When you're not like everyone else, you tend to stand out. But we weren't destructive. And we certainly didn't want to harm anyone."

Nelson didn't comment. Instead, he picked up the police report. "The case seems pretty open and shut."

Mia sighed as disappointment crashed over her. She'd hoped perhaps he might be different because of the way he'd been there for her so far. But he was like the others, despite the sympathy in his voice. She couldn't rely on him to support her or her campaign to free Lindsey. Anger burned away her disappointment in a hot rush. She snatched the report from his hands and stuffed it back in the storage cabinet.

"If Lindsey didn't bring in the butane," he said, forcing her to pause in the act of closing the storage cabinet doors, "then how did her fingerprints get on the canister's remains?"

"I don't know." Mia turned to face him.

He was tall and broad-shouldered. Like a sturdy and solid tree. The kind that wouldn't break in an ice storm. She wanted to trust him, trust in him. She wanted to believe steady confidence would bolster her through the treacherous waters of trying to free Lindsey.

She held his gaze even as she told herself she couldn't depend on him, to do so would only be another bad decision on her part. "Lindsey vows she didn't touch the canisters, or even know they were there."

He gestured toward the storage cabinet. "Witness accounts say they saw Lindsey at the camp stove moments before it blew up. But when the smoke had cleared, she'd been one of the first to get out of the warehouse."

"Like I said, she was nauseous and had gone out to get fresh air." Why wouldn't anyone accept that explanation?

Other witnesses put Mia on the dance floor at the time of the explosion. She had helped many of the partygoers out of the building.

A fact that had helped in her defense.

Mia worried her bottom lip. "The prosecution made the case that she'd left to avoid the explosion she knew was coming. But that's not true. I know it's not. I just can't prove it. Yet."

"Why do you suspect Ron Davies?"

She pulled out another sheet of paper from the storage cabinet. "There were thirty people there that night. Ron Davies was one of them."

Nelson's eyebrows rose. "Okay. But other than the fact that he's your business competitor now, what proof do you have that he started the fire at the warehouse?"

Blowing out an agitated breath, she confessed, "Nothing. I don't like him or how he's been acting. Not really evidence of a crime." She took a beat to collect herself before saying, "There were twenty-seven other people there that night, excluding me, Lindsey and Seaver. It could have been any one of them." As much as she hated to admit it, she couldn't find any clues as to who else would have set the fire.

From one of the drawers of the storage cabinet, she took out the Dillon High School yearbook for that year. "It was high school. The hierarchy was at play. Ron, Kyle, Andy and Xander were the kings of the school." She turned to the page where the four football stars were mugging for the camera. "I suspected that either Andy Walsh or Kyle Long had something to do with the fire until Ron moved back and opened his business and started making my life miserable. Maybe that's clouding my judgment."

"Why those two specifically?"

"Because they were the two witnesses who said they saw Lindsey with the butane canister."

Nelson seemed to contemplate the information. "Tell me about them."

"They were best friends, inseparable. Still are, as far as I can tell. Both grew up around here. Families were close. Lindsey went out on a date with Andy." Mia found a picture of Lindsey in the yearbook. The dark-haired beauty smiled for the camera. Guilt wormed through Mia. Lindsey had so much potential. The world could have been hers. At the very least a home, a family of her own who loved her. Instead, Lindsey only had the four walls of a tiny cell. "All the guys wanted to date Lindsey. She was pretty and sophisticated." Everything Mia wasn't.

"Did something happen that would lead you to believe one of them would set her up for the fire?"

"Other than them lying about seeing Lindsey with the canisters?" She couldn't keep the resentment out of her tone. "Unfortunately, no. And neither one will return my calls or emails."

For a long moment, Nelson was silent. Then he said, "Would you be willing to come to the Rocky Mountain K-9 Unit headquarters with Diesel and me? We can use the FBI resources to look into the fire and into Ron Davies."

Swallowing back her surprise, she didn't hesitate. "Yes. Totally willing."

With a slow nod, he said, "I think we should also pay your friend a visit."

"Lindsey?" Hope flared. Was Nelson really willing to listen to Lindsey's side of the story?

"Yes. Maybe she'll have remembered something about that night that might prove useful."

Mia appreciated his optimism and would take whatever route she could to set her friend free.

The sound of a vehicle pulling up outside drew them to the front window.

"Xander's here." She wondered why he hadn't returned her calls.

"Good," Nelson said, already striding toward the door. "Maybe he can finally confirm your alibi for the car fire."

Mia frowned at Nelson's retreating back. Did he still suspect her of involvement in the car fire? If so, then why offer to help her with the warehouse party fire investigation?

A mix of confusion, dread and frustration bolstered her determination to clear Lindsey's name.

Nelson stepped out the front door of Mia's house and shielded his eyes against the sunlight. He needed a moment. What had he just done?

Offered to take Mia to RMKU headquarters, that was what.

But why?

There was no denying that someone was targeting her and her business. First the shooting, the car accident, someone vandalizing her shed and her dock going up in flames. Clear signs someone was determined to do her harm.

He had a strong belief all of this had to do with the investigation she was conducting into the warehouse fire. But that didn't explain his compulsion to help. The only reason for his wanting to assist that he could comprehend was her unfailing loyalty to her friend. A quality he held in high esteem. He had that same sense of loyalty to his fellow K-9 team members. To his partner, Diesel. And to the men he'd served with as an army ranger. Loyalty meant you had each other's back and a level of trust that went beyond the ordinary.

But could he trust Mia? Or was he being played, like his ex-fiancée had played him?

Alertness slipped over him as Mia joined him on the porch. He slanted her a glance. She barely reached his shoulders. Her short blond hair framed her pretty face while a smile graced her lips, lighting up her eyes and making his chest tighten.

An unfamiliar emotion wormed through him. That smile wasn't for him but rather for her friend Xander.

A silver 4x4 pickup had parked next to Nelson's SUV and behind the old beater of a truck in the gravel drive. A tall, burly man with sandy blond hair climbed out of the driver's-side door and strode toward them. He was wearing cargo shorts and a T-shirt stretched across a wide chest with a fishing gear company logo on the front.

Mia tugged on Nelson's arm. "Come meet Xander."

She led the way down the front porch stairs. She gave the big man a quick, friendly hug. Nelson and Diesel hung back a few paces. Nelson didn't like the way his gut knotted or how Xander kept his hand on her back as she turned to gesture toward Nelson.

"Xander Beckman, this is Nelson Rivers," she said. "And Diesel."

Had she purposely left off Nelson's title of officer?

Xander's focus narrowed slightly as he gave a chin nod of acknowledgement. "Hey." He flicked a glance at Diesel.

Nelson stuck out his hand. "Officer Nelson Rivers with the Rocky Mountain K-9 Unit."

For a moment, Xander just stared at him without moving to take his hand. Nelson kept his stance, waiting. Finally, Xander removed his hand from the back of Mia's low back and gripped Nelson's hand in a firm, beefy grip.

Nelson applied a bit of pressure of his own. Diesel sat at Nelson's side, his gaze intent on the newcomer.

Then abruptly, Xander released Nelson and stepped back. "Why are you here? Is Mia in trouble, again?"

What was it with this town and the people in it always defaulting to thinking the worst of Mia? Was Nelson's judgment being blinded by his attraction to Mia?

EIGHT

Mia let out a huff. "Xander!"

Nelson couldn't stop himself from interjecting with a good dose of irritation lacing his words, "Mia is not in trouble."

Cutting him a quick glance, Xander let out a breath then smiled at Mia. "I was joking."

"I've been trying to call you," Mia said to Xander. "Monday someone shot up the backside of my cabin and today someone set my dock on fire."

Xander's gaze widened. "What? Are you okay?"

"Yep. It was pretty scary," she said in a tone that downplayed how upsetting the event had been. "But Nelson arrived in time to scare the gunman off. And helped put out the flames." She sent Nelson a grateful smile that packed a punch to his solar plexus.

Xander slid his gaze toward Nelson again. Was the anger in his blue eyes directed at the gunman or at Nelson because Xander was jealous of having another male competing for Mia's attention?

Whoa. Nelson wasn't competing for anything.

"Good thing you were around," Xander said. "What brought you here?"

"We're working a case," Nelson told him. "I had questions for Mia."

"Today's Thursday." Xander tilted his head, curiosity evident in his eyes. "Why are you still here?"

Before Nelson could answer, Mia frowned and put her hand on Xander's arm. "I think it was Ron Davies."

Nelson gritted his teeth with frustration. She should not be throwing around accusations until they had proof. "We don't know that is true. But somebody cut Mia's brake line when her vehicle was parked in Ron's lot, and she had to stay the night in the hospital."

Xander covered her hand with his own. "I wish I'd been here to protect you."

"I left messages for you," Nelson stated. "You haven't answered for the past three days."

"I was camping," Xander replied. He looked to Mia. "Remember, I told you."

Mia's face screwed up with confusion. "I don't remember."

Giving her a patient look, Xander said, "That's

okay. No cell service where I was. I saw that you called and came out to see why. Now I know."

"Did you see my calls?" Nelson said, not bothering to hide his annoyance.

"I was planning to return your calls," Xander replied. "You just aren't a priority."

So he had heard his messages. Yet he'd acted like he hadn't recognized Nelson's name when Mia introduced them. Interesting. What was this man's deal?

"Are you ready?" Xander said to Mia with an expectant expression.

She tucked in her chin. "Ready? For what?"

"We had a fishing date for today," Xander told her. "That's the reason I cut my hiking trip short."

"I thought you said you were camping," Nelson said.

Xander's brow furrowed. "Camping, hiking. Same thing." He turned back to Mia. His shoulders slumped. "You forgot."

"I'm so sorry," she said. "There's been so much going on it slipped my mind."

Appearing hurt, Xander released a breath. "I suppose you have had a lot going on. We don't have to go fishing. I can hang out here with you. Keep you safe."

"That's our job," Nelson stated, watching the man closely.

Xander's lip curled for half a second before

his expression cleared and he turned to Mia. His whole demeanor softened. The man obviously had deep feelings for her. "Mia, you don't know this guy. Can you really trust him? Law enforcement? After the way they treated you?"

"He's not like the others," she told him.

Gratified by her declaration, Nelson tried not to let a smile spread across his face. "When did you get back into town?"

Without looking at him, Xander said, "A little while ago."

"Where were you last Friday night?"

That caught Xander's attention. His gaze narrowed on Nelson. "Why?"

"Xander, tell him," Mia insisted.

Darting her a glance, Xander said, "I was home packing for my trip."

"And we talked on the phone," Mia prompted.

"Yeah, we did." Xander shrugged. "Which is when we made our date for today." There was a petulant note in his voice that grated on Nelson's nerves.

"I'm really sorry," Mia said. "I promise we'll go another time."

Xander gave her another soft smile and took her hand. "I'll hold you to that."

Diesel shuffled closer to Mia.

"Nelson's going to help me with my investigation," she told Xander.

Nelson arched one eyebrow. She had shared her investigation with Xander. He tucked the knowledge away.

"Mia, are you still at that?" Xander's exasperation was clear.

"Yes. You know I have to find out the truth," Mia told him. She took a half step away from him, forcing Xander to release his hold on her, which prompted Diesel to move to her side. She rested her hand on his head, her fingers tenderly stroking his fur.

It occurred to Nelson that she took any sort of criticism of her investigation personally. As if the person speaking wasn't just criticizing her need to know the truth but criticizing her. Nelson remembered she'd said her parents were strict. He wondered if they'd also been critical. She'd said she was a disappointment to them, so his guess was, yes. Thankfully, they hadn't broken her. For that, Nelson was glad. He liked her feistiness.

"You've become obsessed," Xander stated. "You forgot I went camping, forgot we had a fishing date. Now you're dragging some stranger—" he gestured toward Nelson "—into the madness."

Hurt filled Mia's eyes. "I thought you understood."

Nelson resisted the need to comfort her.

"I understand obsession," Xander replied softly.

"No!" Mia shook her head. "I'm not obsessed. Lindsey did nothing wrong. *We* did nothing wrong."

Xander reached out and ran a knuckle down Mia's cheek. "I know. I believe in you."

Nelson's fingers curled, though he couldn't have said why. But he didn't like Xander. Or the surge of jealousy filling his veins. Clearly, these two cared deeply for each other. Otherwise, why wouldn't Mia send the guy on his way?

Diesel let out a soft growl, also expressing his displeasure at Xander touching Mia. Nelson wanted to praise the dog. He didn't care for how familiar Xander was with Mia, but Nelson had no say in the matter.

Mia captured Xander's hand, breaking the contact with her cheek. She released his hand to say, "Have you any idea where Andy Walsh and Kyle Long are?"

Nelson watched Xander closely. Xander's eyes flared slightly. Surprise or irritation?

"I didn't keep in touch with them after high school," Xander told her. "I've told you this."

She grimaced. "I know, but I was hoping maybe now that you've been back in town for a while, you'd had contact with either of them or their parents. Or anyone else that might know where they are."

"I have not." Xander gave her a puzzled expression. "Why do you want to talk to them?"

"Because I want to know why they lied about seeing Lindsey with the butane canisters," she said. "They won't communicate with me."

Xander shook his head. "They had no reason to lie."

She turned to Nelson. "Maybe Ron knows how to reach them."

"We'll ask him," Nelson assured her.

"And I doubt Ron has had contact with either of them," Xander interjected.

Nelson held his gaze. "Were you and Ron good friends?"

"I wouldn't say we were best buddies or anything." Xander returned his attention to Mia. Concern etched on his face. "You really need to leave it alone. Lindsey is doing her time. Nothing you do is going to change the facts."

"She's innocent," Mia said, her voice cutting through the air like a knife.

Xander sighed heavily. "I'll be off, then. Maybe we can go fishing this weekend." Without waiting for her to reply he walked back to his truck and left in a cloud of dust.

"Sorry about that," Mia said. "He's usually not so terse. I feel bad about bailing on fishing with him."

Nelson doubted the guy was as upset about the

missed fishing as he was about Nelson's presence. The guy acted like a jealous boyfriend. Yet, from the way Mia talked, she considered him a friend.

Either way didn't matter. Xander's feelings weren't Nelson's concern. Nelson was going to find out who wanted to hurt Mia and he wouldn't let anyone get in the way of that goal.

"We should get going?" The sooner they got to headquarters the better. There they would have the resources to answer some questions, like where were the two men who claimed to have seen Lindsey with the butane canisters. And where was Ron Davies this morning?

She gave a nod and hurried to the cabin to grab her backpack-style purse.

They got into Nelson's SUV and headed out. Diesel pressed against the grating separating him from the front seats. Buckled into the passenger seat, Mia shifted to stick her fingers through the metal holes to rub his snout. His dog clearly liked her.

As they drove, Nelson couldn't help himself from asking, "What's going on between you and Xander?"

"Going on?"

"Are you in a relationship?" He hated the way his breath held, waiting for her answer.

Mia barked out a sharp laugh. "Hardly. Just friends. Like I told you before, he's the only one who stuck by me through the trial and the dark days after during our senior year of high school. But then he left to go to college in California. He only recently returned."

"Did you say Ron Davies recently returned, as well?"

"Ron returned about a year ago from wherever he went off to after high school." There was no mistaking the resentment in her voice. "He opened his company about three months ago. He's decimating my business."

"You don't know where, or if, Ron Davies went to college?"

"No. But that seems like something I should look into."

Her voice held a contemplative tone that made Nelson smile.

"It's something *we* will look into," Nelson told her. And he was rewarded with a smile that brightened her eyes. His chest tightened and a lump formed in his throat. He had to force his gaze back to the road for fear of losing himself in her eyes. "Did you really forget that you had a fishing date?"

"I don't remember agreeing to go fishing with Xander today." Uncertainty underscored her words. "But I've been so stressed. I might have said yes when we talked on Friday. I don't know.

I was pretty upset. All of my reservations for the weekend had canceled."

It seemed odd that she wouldn't remember Xander's camping trip or the arrangements to go fishing, especially when she had a business to run, but she had been under a lot of stress. And stress could play tricks on the mind. Nelson knew this from his time in Afghanistan and on the police force. Not to mention the stress he'd endured learning of Kelsey's affair.

He didn't get why she'd cheat, rather than just break off their engagement. He'd been oblivious when they were together until someone had seen her with another man, a well-known Denver doctor. She'd tried to lie about it, hoping to convince him not to believe the accusation but then he'd found out the truth. Kelsey finally admitted to the affair. He'd called off the engagement and she married the doctor a year later. Go figure.

He slanted Mia another glance, his heart hardening just a bit. He would be a fool to let down his guard around this woman. Around any woman. He was not going to let himself be set up for betrayal again.

"What Xander said about you becoming obsessed…" Nelson began. "There's some truth to that, isn't there?"

"Maybe." The admission came with a good dose of irritation in the single word.

"I promise you, Mia," Nelson said, "I'm going to help you prove or disprove Lindsey's innocence. But whatever we find, you will have to accept. Deal?"

When she didn't respond, he had a sinking sensation in the pit of his gut that she would never give up trying to prove her friend's innocence. And it might just get both Nelson and Mia killed.

As Nelson drove the SUV out of the town of Dillon, the countryside gave way to residential suburbia with the Denver skyline appearing before them. The spring sunlight shone on the buildings, making them gleam. Yet, sitting in the passenger seat and staring out the side window, Mia could hardly appreciate the beauty of the scenery.

While she was grateful for Nelson's willingness to help her, his insistence that she would have to accept whatever they found grated on her nerves. She was the only one who believed in Lindsey's innocence. She wished Nelson believed her, believed in Lindsey.

Once he met Lindsey, he would change his mind. Mia had to believe he was good at his job, and having him on her side, she wouldn't be so alone. She turned to face him. "Do you think we can see Lindsey today?"

He didn't look away from the road. "Once

we're done at headquarters, I'll call the women's correctional facility and make arrangements."

Gratified, she turned back toward the view out the side window. Then quickly faced him again. "Thank you. I do appreciate what you're doing for me, for her." She glanced behind her to the compartment where Diesel rode. Catching her eye, the dog lifted his head. "I appreciate you both."

Nelson flashed her a smile. "No thanks are necessary. We're doing our job. Part of which is to keep you safe."

Of course, she understood Nelson was doing his job, but hearing him say it left her a bit deflated. She wasn't even sure why. Maybe because for the first time in a long time she wasn't alone. Or lonely.

"If the reason someone is targeting you," Nelson continued, forcing her attention back to him, "is because you're investigating a case that's been closed for a decade, then there's a problem."

"You can say that again," she muttered. A big problem because an innocent woman sat in jail while the real arsonist was free.

"But, if this really does have to do with Ron Davies wanting you out of business and not anything to do with the warehouse fire, he's gone too far and he will pay." Nelson's tone took on a steely edge. "Before I confront Davies, I need all the ammunition we can get."

"I understand." She liked that Nelson was thorough. Competent. Smart. She realized with a little start that she trusted him in a way she did few others. And that left her with an off-kilter sensation, much like dizziness after a go on the Tilt-A-Whirl at the county fair.

Nelson regripped his hands on the steering wheel, drawing her focus. He had nice hands, strong-looking, tapered fingers with cared-for nails, but not in a pampered way. She liked that.

"I need to know Ron's movements for every moment when something happened to you." Nelson met her gaze with a quick glance. "Plus, I want to look into these other suspects that you think might be involved."

A jolt of surprise at his unexpected words sped up her heartbeat. "Do you mean all the partygoers? Or just Andy and Kyle?" The latter two were whom she had at the top of her suspect list because they both had left town quickly after the fire and had been so hard to reach. Had they set the fire and were afraid to be caught?

"Andy, Kyle and Xander."

Mia frowned, not liking that he added Xander in with the other two. "Xander didn't do this. He couldn't have. He was my friend then, he's my friend now."

"But was he Lindsey's friend?"

Mia turned the question over in her head.

"There had been no love lost between Xander and Lindsey prior to the fire. I'm not sure why. There were many times when Lindsey and I would hang out and Xander would show up. But the reverse happened as well. It didn't bother me. I liked hanging out with both of my friends. But the two of them always seemed to clash."

"Two strong personalities," Nelson said. "Both of them vying for your attention."

"I suppose," Mia admitted. Uncomfortable with his statement, she wasn't sure why she hadn't realized before the reason her friends were at odds with each other. "I think they both wanted to be in charge." She wrinkled up her nose. "It was high school. Though Xander was a jock and part of the 'in' crowd, he was nice to me."

"It also sounded like he might have had romantic feelings for you even back then."

"Friendship, that's all," she insisted. Though a memory of a stolen kiss surfaced. Xander had taken her to a movie and in the dark had kissed her. She'd laughed, embarrassed and flattered. He'd laughed, too, giving a wink as if to say he was only joking. They'd never talked about it, and he'd never tried to kiss her again. She didn't think of Xander that way. She couldn't. He was her friend. And she needed his friendship.

Nelson slowed the vehicle as they came upon a sprawling campus just outside of the Denver city limits, the big sign out front making it clear where they were. He turned into the Rocky Mountain K-9 Unit headquarters lot, parked and then hustled her and Diesel inside the building.

They bypassed a set of offices, one with a dark-haired woman at her desk and a bigger office with a man talking on the phone. There was a large, vacant conference room straight ahead that they skirted around until they reached the back area where there was an open-plan office space. Each section had a dog kennel. All the desks were empty.

Nelson's space was neat and tidy, with a framed photograph of him in a police uniform standing with an older woman, whom she guessed to be his mother. She had the same bright blue eyes as Nelson.

He put Diesel into his kennel. "Don't worry, boy. We'll be back to get you soon." Nelson then turned to Mia. "I need to check in with my boss. Come with me, I'd like him to meet you."

"You would?" The suggestion of meeting Nelson's boss caused a nervous riot of butterflies to swarm through her.

Nelson cocked his head and gave her a strange look. "Of course. He gave me permission to do what I can to make sure you're safe. I'm sure he'd like to know who you are."

"Are you sure that's a good idea?"

Did the man know of her past? What if Nelson's boss decided she wasn't worth protecting? She wasn't sure she could take any more judgment or rejection at the moment.

Nelson took her hand. "It will be all right."

With him holding on to her, she truly wanted to believe him. But should she?

NINE

Swallowing her nervousness, Mia followed Nelson toward the front of the building to the offices they'd passed on their way in. He knocked on the door to the outer office. An attractive woman with long dark hair and a beautiful smile greeted them with a wave, indicating for them to come on in.

"Hello, Nelson." The woman turned dark eyes on Mia. "And who do you have with you today?"

"Jodie, this is Mia Turner," Nelson replied.

"Ah," Jodie said. Obviously the woman had heard of her. Knowing that only made Mia's nerves stretch tighter.

"Mia, meet the unit's administrative assistant, Jodie Chen. Technically, she's the boss's assistant, but she helps us all out. We couldn't do what we do without her."

The warmth in Nelson's voice made Mia's chest ache slightly. It was clear that he cared for this woman. Romantically? Mentally giving herself a head slap, because Nelson's love life was none of her concern, Mia nodded a greeting.

Jodie waved a hand. "What are you softening me up for?" She trained her dark gaze on Mia. "It's nice to meet you, Mia. I understand you have had some trouble of late."

Mia glanced at Nelson. What had he told them? "Yes. It's nice to meet you as well."

"I'll buzz the boss and see if he's available," Jodie said. She picked up the receiver on the phone and pressed a button. "Nelson and guest to see you."

Visible through the glass wall separating the offices, the man sitting at his desk waved for Nelson and Mia to join him.

Jodie hung up the phone with a grin. "Go on in."

Nelson opened the door to the inner office. Mia moved to follow him as Jodie said, "You're in good hands. Nelson's one of the best. In fact, our whole team is the best. You couldn't have better people at your back."

The reassurance both eased the tightness in Mia's chest and made her throat close with emotions she didn't understand. She gave the woman a thankful smile. "I appreciate you saying so."

Mia walked into the office and joined Nelson behind two chairs facing the desk. A large brindle-coated dog lay on a bed in the corner. He lifted his head for a moment, then relaxed back down with his snout on his paws.

The man behind the desk gestured. "Take a seat."

Mia rounded the end of the chair and sat, her gaze taking in Nelson's boss. His black hair was a little longer on top, which seemed to emphasize his strong, clean-shaven jaw. His eyes were so dark they looked like polished onyx and assessed her with an intensity that made her want to squirm.

"Tyson, this is Mia Turner." Nelson's voice brought her a measure of comfort. She wouldn't want to face Tyson alone.

"I gathered as much," Tyson said. "Miss Turner, I'm Sergeant Tyson Wilkes. Nelson pleaded your case, and we are happy to help."

Her gaze jumped to Nelson. He'd pleaded for permission to protect her? Her heart melted just a little bit more. The guy really was over-the-top in the superhero department. But she couldn't find fault. She liked superheroes. She liked Nelson. She looked back to Tyson. "I appreciate everything that Nelson and Diesel have done."

Tyson gave a nod. His gaze focused on Nelson. "Bring me up to speed."

He proceeded to explain about the attack at the shed and the dock fire, discovering Mia's investigation and her theories that someone other than Lindsey caused the fire and framed her friend.

Tyson's gaze flicked to Mia and once again she resisted the urge to squirm under his regard, because she was unrepentant about her quest to exonerate her friend. She did, however, respect the way Nelson told his boss the details without embellishment or personal opinion. Just the facts. Straightforward and to the point.

"I'm not going to lie to you, Miss Turner," Tyson said, steepling his hands. "It's a long shot at this juncture to prove anything other than what the evidence points to in your friend's case."

"But, sir—" Mia sputtered in protest. Was he going to tell Nelson to stop helping her? Panic flapped like an angry bird in her chest.

Tyson held up a hand, staying her words. "However," he said with emphasis, "we believe no stone should go unturned in any investigation. Someone clearly wants to do you harm. Whether we discover this has something to do with your friend and that fire or something altogether different, we will get to the bottom of the situation and bring the person to justice."

She blew out a breath of relief. Though she wasn't happy with the caveat that suggested she was searching for a needle in a haystack, she did appreciate their commitment.

"Then I am doubly grateful," she told him. She

knew the truth would win out. She lifted up a silent prayer that her confidence wasn't misplaced. Then chastied herself for the smidge of doubt.

"Tyson," Nelson said drawing his boss's attention. "I would like to ask Russ to look at what Mia has gathered. As well as I'd like to talk directly with Lindsey Gates."

Tyson nodded. "If there is something to be found, Russ and his minions will find it."

The two men shared a smile. Mia looked questioningly at Nelson.

"You know that animated movie with the evil genius who has the little funny yellow men doing his bidding?" Nelson asked.

She vaguely knew what he was referring to. "Whatever works."

"Before you head off to talk to Russ," Tyson said, "I'd appreciate it if you would help Sawyer with a training session for the new recruits and their handlers."

"Of course." Nelson turned to Mia. "That is, if you don't mind hanging around for a bit longer. I know we have to get back to your shed to see what repairs need to be done."

"It can wait. You do what you need to do. I'm just grateful for the assistance."

"Wonderful," Tyson said. "Everyone's assembling in the outdoor training yard." He turned to

Mia. "You'll find this interesting. It's not often civilians get to watch our training sessions."

Pleased to be included into a special group, she smiled at the man. "I'm looking forward to it."

Nelson stood. "Thank you."

Mia rose and followed him out of the office. They headed back to Nelson's cubicle, where he released Diesel from the kennel. Nelson gave Mia a quick glance, then grabbed a duffel bag from beneath his desk. He unzipped it and pulled out a thick jacket, handing it to her. "It's not super cold out. But since you won't be moving around, it might be better for you to put this on over your jacket."

"You won't need it?" She hugged the jacket to her chest and inhaled the scent that was him, once again deciding sandalwood was her favorite scent.

"Naw," Nelson said. "I'll be moving around with Diesel."

Grateful for his consideration, she shrugged on the larger coat, then followed Nelson and his partner out a back door to another building, which housed several kennels that had outdoor access to a large fenced-in area. There was a rectangular indoor training ring that was empty at the moment.

"In the winter we train inside but when the weather turns, we do as much as possible outdoors," Nelson explained. He pointed to several open doors. "The trainers' offices and classrooms for the new handlers." He gestured to a closed door with a keypad beside it. "Our equipment storage facility holds a variety of things needed for training as well as gear for the team." He stopped beside three empty kennels. "We have three new one-year-old dogs in training. They must be in the outdoor yard. You'll get to meet them. Rebel is a male Rottweiler. It will be interesting to see how he fares. He's a stubborn guy. Then there's Shiloh, a very sweet male black Lab."

"And the third dog?"

He grinned and started them walking again. "Chase, a beagle. A fireball of energy. Makes me thankful for my more sedate partner."

Agreeing with his assessment of Diesel, she asked, "How long does it take to train a K-9?"

"Months. Each dog will be evaluated throughout the training to determine if they have the skill and drive to excel," he replied and held open a door leading outside.

She stepped past him into a blast of cold wind that ruffled through the short ends of her hair. "And if they don't excel?"

"Some will be trained as service dogs in different disciplines, such as hearing assistance dogs or guide dogs. Some will be returned to the breeder."

"And the breeder's okay with taking them back?"

"Yes," Nelson said. "The three dogs we have now were gifted to the FBI for training by a prominent breeder we were able to protect when the breeder was targeted. If the dogs wash out, the breeder will find a home for them or another service program. Dogs are used for a wide range of purposes. Medical alert for diabetics, and emotional support."

She liked knowing that others had been safeguarded by the K-9 unit. And all the ways that dogs were assets to humans amazed her. She'd never had a dog, or any pet. Her parents hadn't wanted one in the house.

Coming to a stop at the gated fence circling the outdoor training yard, Nelson lifted the latch and opened the gate for her and Diesel. He quickly shut it behind him. There were several people already assembled at one end of the yard. A tall, rugged-looking man broke away from the group and approached them. With him came a beautiful yet intimidating Doberman.

Nelson shook the other man's hand. "Ben, this is Mia Turner. Mia, Ben Sawyer and his K-9, Shadow."

"Nice to meet you." Mia nodded a greeting but edged closer to Diesel when Shadow's dark gaze landed on her. "What does your dog do?"

"Protection," Ben replied. "He has a keen sense of his surroundings and the ability to anticipate danger. The best dog ever." He grinned. "But we all think that about our partners."

That made sense to her because Shadow looked like he could take down a bear.

Ben focused on Nelson. "Heard you would be out of pocket for a while. We didn't expect to see you today, but it would be great for you and Diesel to give the new handlers a demo of your partner's abilities."

"We're ready," Nelson replied.

Another man joined them and introduced himself as Lucas Hudson. His K-9, a sleek border collie with a white chest and black around her eyes, ears and back, was named Angel.

Angel appeared so sweet. "And what does your dog excel at?"

"Search and rescue," Lucas said. "This little one loves the snow."

He clapped Nelson on the back. "So, this is who has been keeping you busy. About time you put yourself back out there."

Mia's cheeks heated at the suggestion there was something personal going on between her and Nelson. She chanced a glance at Nelson and realized, with a little start, that the idea of a relationship with the handsome officer wasn't exactly an abhorrent one. In fact, if circumstances were different, if her life were different, he'd be the kind of man she'd want in her life.

Good thing she knew the difference between fantasy and reality. Nelson was firmly tucked away in the realm of the impossible.

Nelson lifted an eyebrow. "Working a case."

Mia tried not to wince at the label but at least she knew where she stood with him. She stepped away to allow the men to talk but their voices carried.

"Any news on the car fire victim, Kate Montgomery?" Nelson asked, clearly wanting to change the subject.

Lucas and Ben exchanged a glance. "No change. Still in a coma. But the boss had her moved from Boulder to here in Denver, where they are better equipped to handle long-term care."

Mia's heart twisted. She wished she had been able to help the unconscious woman. She returned to Nelson's side. "Sorry to overhear, but I've read that talking to people in a coma is a form of therapy," she said. "Doctors don't know what those in a coma hear and understand, but several people have awoken, saying they remember snatches of conversation."

All three men looked at her with interest.

She smiled and shrugged. "I'm an input junkie." The more obscure the better. She enjoyed learning and had spent many nights down various rabbit holes of information on the internet.

Lucas rubbed his chin. "That's not a bad idea. I'll talk to Tyson about it. I'm willing."

"Mia and I can stop by the hospital on the way out of town," Nelson said.

Mia smiled up at him, pleased that he approved of her idea.

One of the trainers clapped their hands loudly, gathering everyone's attention.

"Sawyer, Rivers," a barrel-chested man with a shaved head called.

"Ha. One of you gets to do the dirty work today," Lucas mocked and wiped his brow.

"Hey, wait a second," Ben said. "I say we draw straws."

"Yeah, just like old times," Nelson said.

Mia liked the camaraderie between the men. They apparently were comfortable with each other.

"Only our backdrop is the Rocky Mountains, not an Afghan desert," Tyson said as he joined them.

All three men straightened and turned toward their boss.

Mia tucked in her chin at the tidbit of info. "Were you all soldiers?"

"Army rangers," Nelson said.

"The boss was our captain," Lucas supplied.

Tyson carried a case that Mia recognized as a gun case.

Tyson must have seen her assessing look. He said, "We use blanks in our demonstrations. It simulates a real scenario, but with none of the danger."

"We wouldn't want to scare the recruits or the dogs before the training even begins," Lucas stated.

"But I'm not wearing the bite suit," Ben grumbled. "I had to last time."

Nelson pointed to the ring where a man in a bite suit, complete with a caged helmet, walked to the center of the yard and halted. "Looks like Jordy, one of the young rookie trainers, drew the short straw today."

"What's so bad about wearing the bite suit?" Mia asked.

"The suit only provides so much protection," Tyson replied.

"He won't get bitten or broken, but he will get bruised," Nelson said.

"Hence we usually draw straws," Lucas interjected.

"Ah. Sounds painful," she commented.

"We all can handle it, though," Lucas said.

She smothered a smile at the male bravado.

"Ben, you and Shadow do your thing," Tyson said. "I'll give this to the trainer." Ben, Shadow,

Lucas, Angel and Tyson walked toward the cluster of people.

Nelson turned to her. "It would be better for you to hang back here. Less chance of being a distraction for the dogs or handlers."

Nelson and Diesel joined the others and conferred with the trainers for a moment, then he and Diesel jogged back. "We'll work with the recruits and the dogs after this demonstration."

"No problem," she said, glad to hang back and watch.

Tyson removed the gun from the case and gave it to Jordy, the man in the bite suit, who tucked it into the belt around his waist. Tyson walked away to stand with the rest of those gathered to watch. Mia assumed they were the recruits and more trainers.

Ben and Shadow walked to a few feet away. Ben gave a hand signal and Shadow lay on the ground. Mia could see the dog still had his feet under him, though his belly was touching the grass.

Jordy started running.

Ben shouted, "Take hold."

Shadow popped to his feet and chased after Jordy, quickly catching up to him. The dog leaped in the air, taking a hold of the back of the bite suit and bringing Jordy crashing to the ground. Jordy grabbed the gun from his waist and aimed off to the side. The gun went off, with a loud bang.

Mia was jolted by the noise, and her breath caught. "That sounded like real gunfire."

"It did. But it couldn't be." Concern laced Nelson's voice.

Obviously, the trainer thought so, too, because he seemed to panic, rolling over, taking Shadow with him. The dog let out a yelp that could only mean pain but still didn't let go, despite the awkward position he and Jordy were now locked in.

Ben rushed over and let out a loud whistle. The dog immediately released his hold on the bite suit and then sank to the grass, panting hard.

Nelson shoved Diesel's lead into her hands. "Okay?"

"Sure." She smiled down at the yellow Lab who sat beside her. "We're good."

Nelson ran to join the others gathered around the downed Jordy and Shadow.

The dog struggled to stand, holding up his left back leg. Ben scooped the dog up into his arms and hurried away.

Mia sent up a quick prayer the dog wasn't seriously injured.

Jordy got to his feet. Tyson took control of the weapon, putting it back in the box. For a few minutes the group talked, no doubt discussing the incident, then Tyson turned and headed back toward the training center, shaking his head the whole way.

Nelson returned, taking Diesel's leash and steering them back into the indoor training center.

Mia asked, "What happened?"

"I don't know," Nelson said. "But there will be an investigation. Unfortunately, Shadow is hurt. He tweaked his hip when Jordy rolled over him."

"Where is Ben taking him?"

"To the local veterinarian, Dr. Sidney Jones. She's real good with the working dogs."

"Are the trainings done?"

"For now," Nelson replied. "Tyson has to figure out what happened. So he canceled today's trainings."

As much as she wanted him to continue to work Lindsey's case, she understood his tension and where his loyalties lay. "I'd understand if you need to stay here and help out. I can catch a bus back to Dillon."

His expression softened. Then he reached out to tuck a lock of her hair behind her ear, the touch gentle and sweet and sending little shivers of delight sliding down her skin. Surprise morphed into a yearning that left her a bit breathless.

Silly of her to long for a connection with this man, yet she couldn't seem to keep the tide from flooding her veins. She stepped back for fear she might do something embarrassing, like throw her arms around him, hang on tight and never let go.

TEN

"There's nothing I can do here," Nelson said, letting his hand fall back to his side.

Mia missed the sensation of his touch. She wanted to take his hand and hold his palm to her cheek. She liked this man way too much. And was becoming too attached. But how could she not? He was kind, considerate and brave. The type of man any woman worth her salt would appreciate.

"Except pray that whatever happened today was an anomaly," Nelson continued. "I trust Tyson. We all do. He'll get to the bottom of this. Until then, we can go on with our plan. We'll take your folders and files to Russ and then visit the women's correctional facility before stopping at the hospital."

She breathed a sigh of relief and instantly guilt at her selfishness constricted her breathing. "If you're sure."

"I am." He put his hand to the small of her

back, the pressure warm and secure, and led her back to his desk. "Let me call the prison and set up an interview time. Visitations for law enforcement are different than the normal visits for civilians. I don't know if I'll be able to finagle your presence at this visit."

She hoped he would be able to. "I take it you don't have to sit in the stuffy cubicle with a plastic barrier between you and speak into a grungy old-fashioned phone."

He shook his head. "No. I sit with her face to face at a table. Our conversation won't be recorded. However, she may want her lawyer present."

"As long as she knows I sent you, she'll talk to you." At least Mia hoped so. She'd spent so many sleepless nights imagining what Lindsey might be going through that a permanent ache resided in her heart.

Nelson sat at his desk and picked up his phone. A few minutes later he had the women's correctional facility on the line. After introducing himself, he said, "I would like to make arrangements to interview one of your inmates, Lindsey Gates." After a beat he looked at Mia. "Inmate number?"

"I have it memorized," she said.

He grabbed a pen and paper, and she wrote it down.

He read it aloud into the phone. "Really? That's too bad. Yes, another time." He hung up.

Mia's breath stalled in her throat. "What happened?"

He turned to face her, his expression grim. "Unfortunately, Lindsey is in solitary confinement for the next forty-eight hours. For fighting."

Mia's heart sank. Guilt swamped her. She held onto the edge of the desk to stay upright.

Nelson jumped to his feet and put his warm hands on her biceps. "Mia."

She looked up into his eyes. The blue was so bright and clear she could see her reflection in his gaze. Had to be a trick of the light? "She shouldn't be there. It's not fair."

"Sometimes life is not fair." He pulled her close, rubbing a hand down her back. "God never promised it would be."

His words brought tears that pricked her eyes. His embrace soothed the riot of emotions inside of her. She clung to him, needing his strength. "I know. Sometimes it's hard to reconcile faith with the injustices of the world."

"Yes, it really is." Nelson's voice held a note of hurt she'd not heard from him before.

Her heart ached to think that somebody had caused him pain.

He released her, stepping away to gather his things and Diesel.

She put a hand on his arm, stilling his movements. "Nelson?"

He stared down at her hand before lifting his gaze to meet hers. For a brief moment there was heartache in the depth of his crystalline eyes, but then he banked the emotion, shuttering his expression and closing her out. She dropped her hand away, and hurt and disappointment balled beneath her breastbone. Clearly, he didn't want to share his pain or let her help him. She was just a job. Nothing more.

Best this way. And she'd be wise to remember that trusting him didn't mean letting herself develop romantic emotions that had nowhere to go.

Pushing past her, Nelson said, "Come on, let's go see Russ."

Nelson could tell Mia was fretting in the passenger seat as he drove them to the FBI forensic lab. No doubt she was worried about her friend. Fighting while in prison was always a disaster. It didn't matter who started the fight; anyone caught was sent to the hole. The prison official hadn't said if there were injuries resulting from the altercation, which led Nelson to hope Lindsey had fared well. But still, he understood how much guilt Mia held on to over Lindsey's imprisonment.

He could only imagine how he'd react if one of

his fellow team members were in trouble. They were like family. They had each other's backs. All of the K-9 officers had been there for him when his relationship with Kelsey had gone south.

Today, seeing Shadow hurt had brought on a deep ache. He sent up a prayer that the dog's injury wasn't severe.

It was very upsetting. That was the only excuse he could come up with for acting so unprofessionally and pulling Mia into his arms.

Though having her close, her cheek resting against his chest, had seemed right, natural. Like she belonged there.

He really needed to take a step back and shore up his defenses. He was becoming emotionally attached to this woman. He glanced at her as she fiddled with the position of her seat belt across her shoulder. How could he help becoming attached? She was brave and kind. Compassionate and thoughtful. Her suggestion to visit Kate Montgomery, the coma victim from the car fire, and talk to her could only come from a place of empathy. He forced his attention back to the road. Now was not the time.

"Nelson, what did Lucas mean when he said it was about time you put yourself back out there?"

Mia's words reverberated through his brain, hitting hard because of what he'd just been thinking. His gaze swung back to her. She sat angled toward him, curiosity and something else he wasn't sure how to define lighting the pale brown depths of her gaze.

Looking back to the road, he was tempted to say that Lucas was just being Lucas and not to put any stock in his ribbing. Yet, the compulsion to confide in her was stronger than he could resist. "It's been a while since I've dated."

"Because someone hurt you?"

He shot her a sharp glance. "What makes you say that?"

"A hunch." She shrugged. "I could be wrong."

"You aren't wrong." But she was perceptive. "I was engaged a couple of years ago. It ended badly." The old wounds ached as if he'd rubbed them with a nail.

"I'm sorry she hurt you." Mia's soft voice was like a caress, soothing over the ragged edges.

"I don't miss her." The admission came as a surprise as he realized the truth of the statement. He thought about her. About her betrayal and how it hurt, and he didn't want to suffer again. But he didn't miss her. Odd, that.

"That's a telling statement," Mia said.

"True." Even odder that Mia could see it. Or maybe not odd. She was a smart, capable woman and she seemed to understand that on some level he was admitting that the love he'd had for Kelsey was gone. Something he'd only just now comprehended.

"If your engagement was over a couple of years ago, why haven't you dated since then?"

The probing question sliced through him, leaving him raw and exposed. He was thankful to pull into the parking lot of the forensic lab. He turned off the engine and faced her. "Because I haven't found anyone I'm willing to take a risk on."

As he gazed into Mia's eyes, the idea that she might be worth the risk sneaked through his consciousness. Whoa. *Get it together, Rivers.*

He unbuckled and then climbed out, needing the cool air to bring some sanity back to his brain. Thankfully, she remained silent as they walked toward the entrance.

Inside the lab, they presented Mia's files to Russ and his team, who promised to do what they could to find as much information as possible on all of the partygoers from the warehouse party fire. And to reexamine the evidence collected by the Dillon police. Russ had apologized for not getting to Nelson's request from before but assured him he'd make it a priority.

Back in the SUV, Nelson's stomach rumbled. They'd skipped lunch. "Let's grab burgers before we head to the hospital to see Kate Montgomery."

"Sounds like a plan," Mia said. "Do you know what the visiting hours are at the hospital?"

"Oh, good thought." He used the Bluetooth to call the hospital and discovered that a physical therapist was working with the unconscious Kate at the moment. The nurse suggested visiting in the morning. Nelson disconnected the call. "When we stop, I'll text Lucas Hudson and let him know that we won't be visiting Kate tonight and that he should go in the morning."

"He's the officer with Angel, the sweet border collie, right?"

Not surprised she remembered the duo, Nelson fought back a poke of jealousy. Lucas always had a way with the ladies. And Angel garnered attention everywhere. "That's right."

"There's a burger joint." Mia pointed to an establishment off to the right. "We can get takeout."

"Good plan." He pulled the SUV into a parking spot.

"I'll order for us," Mia said. "I need to use the restroom."

"I'll take a cheeseburger with bacon. Fries. And Diesel will take a vanilla ice cream cone."

Mia laughed. "He eats ice cream?"

"It's his special treat." Nelson handed her some money.

"I got it," she said, waving away the offer.

He watched her walk inside. He let Diesel out

to wander the nearby strip of grass while he shot off a text to Lucas. Lucas replied quickly, saying he was on it.

Mia returned with their meals in white paper to-go bags. They ate at an outside table.

The sound of Mia's laugh when Diesel gobbled down his treat settled in the vicinity of Nelson's heart.

Back on the road, the late afternoon sun warmed the inside of the SUV. Soft jazz radio played through the speakers. Nelson glanced at a dozing Mia. The bruises to her face from the airbag were already fading. She really was a pretty woman.

The sound of a big motor revving had Nelson glancing in the rearview mirror. A large semitrailer truck, with its high beams on, tailgated the SUV as they rolled down I 70.

Irritation flared within Nelson and he flashed his brake lights, hoping to get the guy to back off.

Instead, the semitrailer inched even closer.

Heart pumping with adrenaline, Nelson stepped on the gas, and the SUV shot forward. But the semitrailer stayed on them. Keeping the pedal depressed, Nelson veered into the left lane. The semitrailer followed suit, disregarding the traffic around them, and the bigger vehicle's bumper clashing with the SUV's. Diesel barked as the grating sound filled the interior.

Mia sat up and gripped the dashboard. "What's happening?"

"This guy behind us—" Nelson ground out, barely willing to voice the suspicion that the maniac was trying to cause them to wreck.

Knowing up ahead was a sharp turn after the Silverthorne Bridge, Nelson wracked his mind for a solution. If they kept up this speed over the bridge and into the turn, there was no question of a crash.

Sending up a prayer of protection, Nelson spied an opening in the traffic of the right lane and yanked the wheel of the SUV, squeezing in front of a luxury SUV. The driver honked.

The semitrailer tried to muscle his way behind Nelson. More honking from the disgruntled luxury SUV.

Off to the right, drawing closer with every second, was a runaway truck ramp.

At the last possible moment, Nelson steered the SUV for the sand-filled incline. The semitrailer braked hard but couldn't make the ramp and zipped past, leaving Nelson's SUV to come to a sinking halt a quarter way up the steep slope.

He turned off the engine and jumped out, his hand on his weapon.

But the threat had disappeared down the highway.

Nelson leaned against the side of the SUV, his

breath coming in shallow gasps. Mia had climbed out and came around to his side.

She placed a hand on his biceps. "You okay?"

"Yeah," he managed to say as he straightened.

Maybe it was the shared trauma of the chase or the adrenaline still pumping through his veins, but he couldn't stop himself from pulling her close and placing his lips on hers.

Shock gave way to sweet sensation as Mia melted into Nelson's kiss. The thrum of fear from nearly being run off the road by the semitrailer truck abated under the onslaught of rioting emotions coursing through her veins. She snaked her arms around Nelson's neck, pulling him closer, deepening the kiss.

With her eyes closed, her head filled with the sandalwood scent she'd come to love. The world seemed to shift beneath her feet.

Nothing had prepared her for this. The few times she'd ever been kissed in the past paled in comparison to Nelson's kiss. This was what poets wrote about, or so she imagined. The intoxicating awareness of their hearts beating in time. Their breath mingling. Their lives intertwined. Could one kiss change everything?

She didn't know the answer and at the moment she didn't care. All she wanted was to revel in the touch of his lips against hers, his hand smoothing out a warm trail down her back, her fingers threading through the short ends of his hair, loving the texture and the way the strands glided across her skin.

The high-pitched whine of sirens approaching barely penetrated through the foggy haze Mia found herself entrenched within.

As the pressure against her mouth eased, she protested with a growl in her throat, pulling him closer. He complied, deepening the kiss. For this moment in time, this was all she wanted, all that mattered. She didn't want to face the reality that someone was trying to kill her and in doing so almost killed Nelson and Diesel.

Finally, Nelson tore his mouth from hers, breathing hard as he dropped his forehead to hers. "I'm sorry," he said. "That was…"

"Yes, it was wonderful," she said. Hoping he was thinking the same. "Don't apologize."

He lifted his head, a smile playing at those glorious lips. "Wonderful." Then his gaze darkened. "And unprofessional."

He stepped away, leaving her to wrap her arms around her middle, already missing the close embrace of his arms. Within the shelter of his hold, she'd understood for a moment what it was to be safe, cared for. Her heart rate slowed to a thud, after the pulse-pounding excitement of his kiss, no doubt.

Illusions.

She wasn't special. Or cared for. The kiss didn't mean anything. Did it?

Nelson turned to meet the oncoming state police cruiser that stopped at the bottom of the incline. Mia took a step, the deep sand of the emergency ramp shifting beneath her feet. The irony wasn't lost on her. Her life at the moment was as precarious and unpredictable as the layers of sand meant to stop a runaway truck. Could it stop her runaway life?

Nelson considered kissing her unprofessional.

She considered kissing him the best decision ever.

But one they couldn't, shouldn't, repeat.

Because of her, Nelson and Diesel were in danger. She had to let them go. Resolve settled over her like a heavy coat. Distancing herself was exactly what she intended to do. She couldn't put anyone else's life in jeopardy because of her.

Shoving away the sharp pang of loss, she joined Nelson and Diesel as they slowly made their way down the incline to talk to the state patrol officer. After Nelson identified himself and explained the situation, she gave her statement to the trooper while Nelson checked on the luxury

SUV the semitrailer truck had hit. It appeared the occupants were safe.

"We'll call you a tow truck," the state trooper said.

"I'd appreciate that," Nelson said. "But it may take a while for the tow truck to arrive. Could you give us a lift into Dillon?"

"Yes, sir."

"I need to get my gear," Nelson said. He turned to Mia, his gaze softening. "I'll be right back. You'll be safe with the trooper."

She nodded, marveling over his continued concern for her well-being. Keeping her safe and protected shouldn't be his responsibility.

A few moments later, Nelson returned with a duffel bag and her backpack-style purse. She'd been so caught up in the situation that she'd completely forgotten about it. Not that she had much of value to carry around with her, but still. Grateful for his thoughtfulness, she took the bag. Their fingers brushed against each other, creating a sweet sort of friction that resonated through her like an electric shock.

Forcing herself to push away her attraction to the handsome officer, she climbed into the back of the trooper's cruiser.

A Denver police cruiser rolled up. Mia waited as the trooper and Nelson spoke to the officers, then joined her in the trooper's vehicle. He rode up front, leaving her and Diesel the back seat. Mia sat as close to the door as possible, giving Diesel enough room where he sat on the seat. The drive to Dillon was silent. The dog laid his head on Mia's lap. She absentmindedly stroked his fur.

How was she going to get Nelson to relinquish control and let her figure this out on her own? It wasn't like he didn't have other matters that he could be attending to. Surely his boss would want him back on his regular assignments. That was her solution. She would call Nelson's boss, Tyson, and ask—no, demand—that he tell Nelson to return to their headquarters. That way Mia wouldn't be responsible for anyone getting hurt.

When they arrived back at her cabin, she headed straight inside to the landline in the kitchen while Nelson let Diesel roam the area just outside the cabin, checking for skulkers *and* keeping close to her, she knew. From a drawer she dug out Nelson's card that he'd given her that first night. On the front was the Rocky Mountain K-9 Unit headquarters' phone number. On the back, he'd written his cell phone number.

Her heart ached, but this was what she had to do. She dialed the headquarters' number. The assistant, Jodie Chen, answered.

"Hi Jodie, this is Mia Turner. I'd like to speak with Sergeant Wilkes, please."

"Of course," Jodie replied. "Is everything okay?"

Afraid to be talked out of her mission, Mia said, "Yes. I need to speak with Sergeant Wilkes."

"One moment." Jodie put Mia on hold.

A few seconds later, Tyson came on the line. "Miss Turner."

Butterflies danced a riotous jig within her tummy, but Mia plunged headlong into her request. "Sir, I need you to take Nelson off this detail. Call him back to headquarters."

There was a long moment of silence. "Did he do something unprofessional?"

Her stomach dropped. Her mouth dried. The sensation of Nelson's lips on hers was imprinted on her brain. "No, sir." Nothing she hadn't wanted to happen.

And unfortunately, that was the problem.

ELEVEN

"It's just, well, sir—" Embarrassment washed through Mia, but she plunged along. How did she explain without sounding ridiculous? "We were almost run off the road today and I can't be responsible if something happens to Nelson or Diesel. I need them to leave."

Another moment of silence followed her pronouncement. "Am I understanding you correctly? Your life is in danger, and you are afraid that Nelson and/or Diesel will get caught in the crossfire?"

She breathed out a sigh of relief. He understood. "Yes, sir. That's exactly my concern."

"I appreciate you calling me with this," Tyson said. "You do realize this is what Nelson and Diesel signed up for?"

"No, sir," she argued. "They signed up to work arson cases, not babysitting me and put their lives in danger."

"Would you prefer I put a different K-9 officer and handler on your detail?"

Everything inside of her rebelled at the suggestion. She couldn't imagine trusting anyone but Nelson. "No, sir. I'd prefer that you all just forgot about me and let me deal with this on my own."

"Not going to happen, Miss Turner." Tyson's voice took on a hard edge.

She made a face, glad that he couldn't see her. "Why not? I didn't ask for this protection."

"And yet, you're going to be protected." Tyson's tone was firm. "If you'd prefer that protection to be at more of a distance, I can tell Nelson and Diesel to retreat to the perimeter of your property."

Frustration had Mia curling her fingers. "Are you all so stubborn?"

A chuckle greeted her question. "You have no idea. I'd like to speak with Nelson."

Mia rolled her eyes and turned toward the archway of the kitchen, intending to call out to Nelson, only to find him standing there, a look of hurt, disappointment and resolve etched into his features. She winced. Obviously, he'd overheard her side of the conversation. Diesel sat beside him, and the dog cocked his head at her. Was that disappointment in his eyes, as well?

Swallowing her embarrassment and frustration, she held out the receiver to him. "Your sergeant would like to talk to you."

Nelson ate up the distance between them with his long legs. He took the phone from her grasp, his eyes never leaving hers. "Yes, boss?"

Unnerved, Mia moved to Diesel's side and crouched down to hug the dog. Nelson was silent, obviously listening to the sergeant talk.

Mia took Diesel's sweet yellow face between her hands and stared into his dark brown eyes, nearly touching noses. "You do know this is the right thing," she said to the dog in a low tone. "I couldn't live with myself if something happened to you…" She threw a glance toward Nelson, who arched an eyebrow at her. She lowered her voice even more. "Or him."

Nelson broke eye contact and stared out the window over the sink. "I understand. You can count on me." He hung up the receiver.

Mia braced herself, expecting him to explode. Instead, he stood with his back to her for a long moment. Finally, he swiveled to face her. His expression had cleared and was now unreadable. "You're not getting rid of us that easily. We are going to see this through. Whoever is after you also came after me and Diesel. I won't stand for it. And I won't stand for you getting hurt."

Part of her wanted to howl in protest. She'd known they were putting themselves in danger for her sake all along, but today just amplified the fact. But a small part of her, a part she was reluctant to acknowledge, cheered. He wouldn't abandon her. She tried to shove the giddy happiness inside her brain into a box. But it wouldn't quite fit. It spilled out, demanding attention. She was falling for the lawman and his dog and there wasn't anything she could do to stop the descent. She could only pray she landed softly and not with a splat.

After a tense and terse evening walking on eggshells around Mia, both of them circling each other like caged animals, Nelson finally retired to the bedroom that used to be Jem's.

Nelson looked at the pictures decorating the walls of the room, focusing on the ones of Mia as a child. Tenderness filled his heart. The young Mia had the same feisty look in her eyes as the grown woman had now. Sadness invaded Nelson. She'd had her whole life ahead of her and then one incident, one horrible tragic night, had derailed everything. What had been her dreams prior to the fire that had claimed one life and put another behind bars?

Had Mia always wanted to take over for Jem? Did she miss being a private investigator? She'd said she'd come home when Jem became ill. But she never returned to her life after he passed.

Instead, she'd focused her efforts on exonerating her friend.

Nelson admired Mia so much, and he feared for her life.

Kissing her had been a glorious mistake. Holding her so close, their lips touching, their breaths mingling, her heart beating next to his, had nearly buckled his knees. The emotional connection with her was beyond anything he'd experienced with anyone else. It scared him almost as much as having that semitrailer truck bearing down on their SUV.

He cared for her deeply. And if he weren't careful, there was no denying that he could fall in love with this woman. He was attracted to her, yes, but there was so much about her he liked and he enjoyed her company.

And then to have her try to finagle his boss into calling him off. Little did she understand that the K-9 unit had been formed out of men and women who not only viewed protecting others as their duty, but as their calling in life. His boss had, in no uncertain terms, made it clear that he was not to let Mia run him and Diesel off. That no matter how much she believed she could handle the danger plaguing her, she needed to be protected. Nelson totally agreed. Tyson had tasked Nelson not only with the duty, but to detect what exactly the person wanting to harm Mia was after. The only way to do that was by keeping her close.

He was not leaving Mia, but he sure wouldn't be kissing her again.

He resolved to stay professional, unemotional and detached. Bury his affection and care for her as much as possible. But as he turned out the light, knowing Diesel was just outside his door, ready to give a warning, Nelson had a sneaking suspicion that his resolve was as unreliable as a boat with holes and would sink out of sight if given the chance.

The next morning, Nelson and Mia shared a light breakfast of coffee and toast, their interaction minimal and awkward. Nelson didn't like the invisible wall between them. He missed the easy way they'd been before the kiss and her call to his boss. But it couldn't be helped. He kept his resolve in place, knowing he needed to stay focused.

Protect Mia, nothing more.

Shadowing her as she went about her chores, Nelson followed Mia down a path to the shed through the trees. The crisp spring air around them was scented with the earthy smells of the forest. The snowfall from the weekend had melted away, but there was more forecasted for the following week. That was life in the high country of Colorado.

Their mission today was to repair the damage done to her equipment. Nelson had a scrub brush and a mixture of vinegar and baking soda to scour away the word *FELON* from the wall inside the shed. He went straight to work, pouring his frustration at whoever was behind the attacks into his efforts to erase the offending word.

Diesel sat in the doorway of the shed, keeping a look out. Nelson had every confidence the dog wouldn't let anyone close without sounding an alarm.

At the sound of Mia struggling behind him, he turned to find her attempting to lift a canoe on a long wooden table. Why wasn't she asking for help? Always so stubborn and independent. Part of her charm. But also irritating. Quickly, he set down the scrub brush and hurried to help her.

She glanced at him with a small smile of thanks.

Staring at the holes in the bottom of the vessel, he asked, "How will you fix this?"

She held up a package. "Quick Patch. Thankfully, I ordered way more than I would need for the coming summer. It's pretty easy. I clean the area and slap this on, then let it sit in the sun to cure."

"Sounds like you've had to repair holes a few times," he said.

"I have," she replied. "You'd be surprised how many people have run a canoe or kayak onto the rocks."

He examined the perfectly round holes, a cold chill settling in his bones. "Yeah, but these weren't caused by a rock."

"No. They weren't." Her tone was flat. Accepting? Or frightened?

His determination solidified. He'd protect her if it was the last thing he did. He left her to repair the canoe and went back to scrubbing away the red letters on the wall.

Sometime later he heard her ask, "Can you help me with this?"

Pleased that she wasn't struggling to do something on her own, he moved to lift one end of the canoe and together they carried it out to the grassy slope, setting it upside down so the patch could dry.

"What's next?" he asked.

"The kayaks," she said. "The jerk ruined two of my four."

"That's because we got here in time before he could do more damage," he said as he followed her back to the shed. He sent up a silent prayer of thanks that they had. This was her livelihood and someone was determined on destroying it and her.

"Yes, I am very thankful that he didn't do more damage." She shook her head. "I don't know what he hoped to accomplish. I have no reservations this week."

"You said Ron Davies had been leaving bad online reviews," he said. "Do you have proof that it's him?"

"No," she replied. "But who else could it be?"

"I will ask Russ to look into the IP addresses of those comments and reviews. We'll get to the bottom of this."

"I appreciate your confidence," she said. "But I'm not holding my breath you'll be able to trace them to him."

He stopped. "You can't give up."

"I'm not going to." She stopped also, then her shoulders slumped. "It's just—" She shrugged and faced him. "It's always been a struggle. Maybe the best thing for me to do is to leave town. Start over somewhere fresh."

Her statement sent a wave of shock through him. Her giving up on her business, on her friend, was incongruent with the person he had come to know. Her determination and loyalty were so attractive, and he couldn't imagine her betraying the commitments she had worked so hard on. "Can you do that?"

She licked her lips, the tiny movement drawing his gaze. "No. Not until I free Lindsey."

His stomach twisted. On the one hand, he was glad to know he wasn't wrong about her, and yet, he hoped she'd consent to the deal he had proposed that she would have to accept whatever outcome the forensic team found, whether it proved or disproved her friend's innocence. That same determination he admired could ultimately be Mia's downfall. Would she chase the theory that Lindsey was framed for the rest of her life, leaving no room for anything else? Anyone else?

Not liking the direction his thoughts were headed, he said, "I'm done with the wall. I can repair one of the kayaks if you walk me through how to do it as you repair the other one."

"Sounds like a good plan." For the next couple of hours, they worked side by side, standing between the two kayaks. Every move she made, he emulated as she talked him through putting on the patch. When they were done, they transferred the kayaks out into the sun. The water looked inviting and peaceful. A bird swooped overhead and dipped down, plucking something from the water, then rising fast and disappearing over the horizon.

"Would you like to go out? We can take a canoe or the other two kayaks."

He turned to Mia, finding her questioning gaze

and liking the way the sunlight heightened the color in her cheeks and the pale brown hue of her eyes.

Floating in the kayaks would allow them to be together, yet separate. But also sitting targets.

He had his weapon and at least they could slip into the water, using the kayak for cover, and swim away if the person trying to hurt her came after them.

Considering how well they worked together and how much he'd been aware of her every breath, some space would be good. "Let's get those two kayaks out."

"First, let's grab some food," she said. "We can take a picnic out to one of the islands."

"Uh, sure." A picnic. Like a date. No, not a date. Just two people out on the water, stopping to eat lunch and then back on the water. Nothing untoward about that.

After packing sandwiches, chips and cold water, Nelson donned the life vest Mia handed him.

"I always keep spares at the house," she said. "I've had customers steal them, so I try not to put them all out."

"Smart of you," he commented, grateful she even had one for Diesel.

Soon they were seated in their one-person kayaks, with Diesel wedged between his knees and facing outward, eager for an adventure. Using the oar, Nelson pushed away from the shore. He gripped the paddle, slipping the blade into the water and pulling, propelling the kayak forward. It was peaceful out on the lake as the vessel slipped silently through the water; the only sounds were the birds in the trees and Diesel's excited panting.

Nelson kept pace with Mia as they glided through the water. Eventually, she guided them toward a small body of land. They beached the kayaks on the shore. Diesel jumped out and ran into the woods.

"Is there anything I should be worried about for Diesel?" Nelson asked Mia as he carried the small cooler they'd packed and strapped to her kayak, to where she spread out a blanket.

"No, he's free to wander." She sat down, pulling the cooler close and popping the lid. "There's nothing that would be a danger to him."

Folding himself into a sitting position, he stretched his legs out and leaned back on his elbows. Overhead, the clouds floated across the blue-gray sky. The expansive mountain views surrounding the lake were enough to take his breath away. It was so peaceful here.

Diesel burst from the bushes and skidded to a halt, sniffing at the cooler. Nelson snapped his fingers. Diesel rounded the blanket and plopped down beside him. Nelson's tension eased to have his dog settled on one side of him and a beautiful woman on the other. They were just two people needing some downtime—there wasn't any reason to make more of this moment than that. And if he kept that in mind, maybe noticing the way the sunlight danced off Mia's platinum blond hair or the way her toned legs drew his attention wasn't such a bad thing. He lifted his gaze to her face, tracing the straight line of her nose, the contours of her cheekbones and her well-shaped lips. So pretty. "Do you come out here often?"

"When I lead a tour around the lake, we'll stop here for lunch or a snack. But this little island isn't as popular as some of the others, which is why I prefer it. It's wild and untamed. A perfect spot." She offered him a sandwich.

"I agree, perfect." Though whether he meant the island or her, he wasn't about to examine. Sitting upright, he took the offered food and unwrapped the ham and cheese on sourdough. "How many islands are there?"

"There are over a dozen, ranging from small, like this one, to medium-sized. There's even one with a mini lake in the middle. We could paddle there next if you want." She took a bite of her sandwich.

"I'm content here," he murmured and ate his sandwich.

They shared the chips and drank their water, then spent time exploring the island, though there wasn't much to it. Nelson realized he was having fun. He couldn't remember a time when he'd been so at ease with someone or had such an enjoyable day.

They decided to paddle around the lake some more before heading back.

By the time the sun started its descent over the horizon, Nelson was ready to return to dry land. A mosquito buzzed around his ear, and he swatted it away. "We should head back," he called to Mia.

She waved her paddle, then maneuvered her kayak in a new direction. He followed her pattern. They glided through the water at a steady pace. The scorched dock and the equipment shed appeared as they came around a bend in the shoreline. And beyond, through the trees, he could make out the A-frame structure of Mia's cabin.

"Race you," Mia challenged. She didn't wait for his reply but put on the speed, quickly drawing away from him.

He laughed. "You're on!" He dug the blades into the water. His muscles burned from the excursion, but the physical activity was welcome.

The sun dipped below the tree line, casting long fingers of shadow across the lake. The growl of a motorboat filled the air, drawing closer with every second. Nelson twisted in the molded kayak seat to see a large three-tube pontoon boat with a canopy speeding toward them, faster than the lake's posted speed limit. Lifting his paddle high, Nelson waved it in the air, hoping to get the driver's attention.

A bright searchlight blinked on, blinding him. The pontoon boat roared past him, causing a wake that rocked the kayak. Nelson grabbed Diesel's life jacket and hung on as they rode the wave.

The pontoon boat aimed straight for Mia, who was also waving her paddle in the air, but the driver clearly wasn't going to stop.

Fear exploded inside Nelson. "Watch out!"

Before the boat reached her, Mia's kayak tipped over and she disappeared beneath the water. The heavy pontoon boat ran over the top of her kayak with a shriek of fiberglass on fiberglass.

Nelson's heart thudded in his ears. Panic roared in his veins. He scrambled in the tight seat to draw his weapon, but the pontoon veered in a wide circle far from Nelson's kayak and returned the way it had come. Nelson couldn't get a good look at the driver because he was wearing a fishing hat pulled low over his ears, sunglasses and a green fishing vest.

Diesel whined. Nelson quickly changed gears,

grabbing his cell phone and dialing 911. Putting the phone in his lap on speaker, he paddled for all he was worth toward the downed kayak as he relayed their need for help to the operator.

He had to save Mia. "Please, Lord, don't let her drown."

TWELVE

The cold lake water penetrated through Mia's clothing, taking her breath away. As soon as she realized the pontoon boat, sporting Ron Davies's logo on the side, wasn't going to veer to avoid colliding with her kayak, she'd shrugged out of her life vest, capsized the kayak and released herself from the vessel.

She swam downward to avoid being ripped apart by the pontoon's motor. The sound of the blades running over the top of the fiberglass kayak above filled her ears with a loud roar and sent a shudder of dread through her.

Concentrating on listening to the boat, she swam in the opposite direction. Her lungs were fiery with lack of oxygen, but she forced herself to keep swimming underwater until the sound of the pontoon motor faded and the world quieted.

Desperate for air, she headed to the surface, kicking her feet and using her hands to propel her upward through the water. She hit the surface, gasping for breath. She swiveled, searching for Nelson, praying the pontoon hadn't run him over.

There he was. He and Diesel were at the remains of her kayak. Nelson looked as if he were about to dive in the water. "Nelson!"

His head lifted at her call. He sank back into his seat. "Mia!"

She waved and pointed toward the shore. Seeing him paddling, she set off, swimming hard and fast, knowing she would come out on the rocks about a hundred yards south of her dock and shed. She clawed her way over the rocks, her numb hands barely registering the small cuts and scrapes from sharp edges of the rocky outcrop.

The scrape of Nelson's kayak hitting the rocks was a welcome noise, despite knowing the damage being done to the vessel. She sat on a large boulder, wrapping her arms around her knees as chills wracked her body. Nelson released Diesel and the dog scrabbled over the rocks to her side. Shivering, she held the Lab close, taking some of his heat into her body.

Nelson lifted the kayak over his head and carried it across the rocks. A feat that had Mia holding her breath. If he slipped...

He didn't. She released the air trapped in her sore lungs. He set the kayak down on the dirt nearby and then he was at her side, gathering her in his arms. "I thought I'd lost you."

She clung to him for a moment while a tremor ran the length of her. Her teeth clattered. A prayer of thanksgiving filled her heart. She was alive and relatively unharmed. Nelson and Diesel were okay as well. God had kept them safe.

"Come on. We need to get you inside and dry." He picked her up, cradling her in his strong arms. "I'll come back for the kayak later."

Snuggling close, already drowsy from the effects of his heat warming her from the inside out, she said, "I doubt anyone will steal it."

She laid her head on his shoulder as he carried her all the way back to her cabin. Diesel ran ahead and sat at the cabin's front door.

"Key in my pocket," she managed to say.

Nelson set her on her feet on the porch but held onto her, supporting her as she dug out the key. He took it from her cold-numbed hands and opened the door. It took effort to make her legs cooperate as she leaned heavily on Nelson, allowing him to guide her inside.

"You're bleeding," he said, grabbing her hands and staring at the lacerations caused by the rocks she had to climb over to get out of the water.

Her jeans were ripped and blood also soaked through from a gash on her knee. "I better go clean up."

"A warm shower," he said. With an arm around her waist, he helped her up the stairs to the bathroom. She rested against the wall while he turned on the water.

He hesitated and she shooed him away. "I'll be fine. Just need to warm up and wash away the grime. You should do the same."

He left and twenty minutes later, she had returned to a more normal state of being. She'd toweled her hair dry and put on fresh warm pants and a thermal shirt. She tucked her feet into a snuggly pair of slippers. The cuts and scrapes on her hands needed more than a Band-Aid like the one she'd put over the gash on her knee, so she wound small towels around them.

She went downstairs and found Nelson had also changed into black sweats and a long-sleeve T-shirt. His hair was damp and his jaw clean-shaven. She tried not to stare.

Diesel was happily eating dry food from a bowl.

Nelson noticed her standing by the stairs and hurried forward. He gently took her hands and removed the towels to inspect her injuries. The little cuts and gashes on her palms and fingers continued to bleed.

"I have a first aid kit underneath the kitchen sink," she told him. "I think I need gauze."

"I'll get it." He pulled her to the couch and urged her to sit. She pressed the towels back to her wounded hands as Nelson hurried to get the first aid kit.

Using her thumb, which seemed the only place that didn't have a cut, she depressed the remote control button, turning the TV on for the evening news.

Nelson returned and sat on the coffee table facing her. He carefully tended to the wounds on her hands, putting ointment over the cuts and scrapes and wrapping gauze over her palms, making a nice little knot of the ends.

"How did you learn to do that?" she asked.

"We had lots of training in the army," he told her.

"How long were you overseas?"

"We did two tours."

Remembering the camaraderie between Lucas, Ben, Tyson and Nelson, she said, "You and your boss and the two handlers I met yesterday, right?"

"And others. Tyson recruited many of those we served with into the K-9 unit."

There was a sadness that seemed to flash in his eyes. And an answering ache flashed through her heart. She could only imagine the torment of what he'd seen during his time in service.

As he finished tying off the second gauze strip on her other hand, she said, "Did you lose many of your friends over there?"

"Yeah, there were casualties." He said it as if trying to distance himself from the pain of his words. "But one that could have been avoided. It was heartbreaking to lose our youngest member, Dominick Young."

She placed the uninjured backs of her hands on his palms. "I'm so sorry."

"It was hard on all of us, but mostly on Tyson," Nelson said. "As our leader, he held himself responsible for Dominick's death."

She could understand that. Just as she would be responsible if anything happened to Nelson or Diesel. She removed her hands, placing them on her lap. "Did you see the driver of the pontoon?"

He stared down at his hands for a moment, then curled his fingers into fists. "Male. But that's all I could tell." He ran a hand through his hair, leaving grooves. "He's bold and determined."

"That was one of Ron's pontoons," she told him. "I only caught a glimpse of it before I capsized, but I saw the logo."

"When I watched you flip, I feared you'd drown."

His voice came out deep with emotions she dare not wonder about, but made her want to hug him close all the same. But she'd become good at shoving such wants aside, so instead, she said, "I was afraid he'd go after you and Diesel."

Nelson huffed out a breath. "No. The attack was solely directed at you, and I couldn't stop it."

The recrimination in his voice had her placing her gauze-covered hands on his again. "Not your fault."

"In the morning, we'll be paying Ron Davies a visit," Nelson stated. "And this time, I won't be so nice."

Her gaze went to the television, snagging on the picture of the blonde hiker that had gone missing. "Can you turn that up?"

Nelson grabbed the remote and moved to sit on the couch next to her. He increased the volume just as the anchor reporting the news said, "The body of Emery Rodgers was found today."

Mia's heart sank. She always hurt when she heard of hikers who'd lost their way and perished.

The anchor continued, "The initial reports are that the young woman was strangled."

Mia gasped.

Nelson's expression turned grim. "I imagine our team will be called in to help search for the suspect."

"You'll have to go?" Even though yesterday she'd wanted that very thing, now panic bubbled up and sweat broke out on the back of her neck at the hint of him leaving.

"Not us," Nelson told her, his gaze pointed.

"Good." She let the word out before she could sensor herself.

His eyebrows rose. "Glad to hear you say that."

Heat infused her cheeks. Did he suspect she had developed romantic feelings for him? Did she want him to know?

Better to let the subject linger between them than deal with messy emotions. Maybe someday... She nearly snorted aloud. "Someday" dreams weren't something she was free to contemplate. Not while Lindsey sat in a jail cell.

"Do you really think that Russ and his team will be able to find something that we can use to exonerate Lindsey?"

Nelson gave her a small smile. "They are the best. I know Russ will do everything he can to determine if the original investigation was on point or not."

Mia knew that it wasn't; however, she wasn't going to argue with Nelson right now. She'd wait to see what the forensic team found. "Let's go talk to Ron Davies now."

Nelson shook his head. "Not tonight. In the morning. Right now, we need to eat and rest. And I need to do a little more digging into Ron Davies. I'll call Russ and see what he's found out."

Her shoulders drooped as if a heavy blanket had been placed around her. "I hate this helplessness," she said. "All of my investigative notes are with Russ. I can't even go over them. Maybe I should start from scratch."

"If it is going to help you sleep, then maybe get paper and pen and write everything out that you can remember. We can talk it through."

As she stared into Nelson's clear blue eyes,

Mia's breath hitched. He somehow always managed to say the right thing. She could easily love this man. His tender care, his willingness to help, his bravery and courage. The overpowering emotion made her want to weep, because she knew a relationship between them wouldn't go anywhere. Eventually, he'd leave her like everyone else. She was grateful he was here now, but she had to shore up her defenses and not fall in love with him. Doing so would only break her heart.

Suddenly, drained from her unscheduled swim and the riot of thoughts and emotions coursing through her veins, she said, "I'm tired. I'll think I'll just go to bed."

"Not before you eat," Nelson insisted. "You sit back and relax. I'll make us something."

Being taken care of was an oddity. Even when Jem was alive, she was the one who had taken care of him. Cooked and cleaned, made sure he was taking his medications. She told herself to enjoy having someone show her such kindness and compassion, because eventually, Nelson would return to his life and she would be alone once again.

Nelson rummaged around the kitchen, finding a can of chicken noodle soup in the back of a cupboard. He checked the expiration date and was glad to see it was still good. He suspected

Mia didn't exactly take care of herself and she deserved to be taken care of. She was so kind and generous. Loyal to a fault. Yet, she kept everyone at arm's length. Even him, when all he wanted to do was help.

He opened the can and dumped the contents into a pot and put bread in the toaster. The mundane tasks kept his thoughts centered.

But as he waited for the soup to warm and the bread to crisp up, he leaned against the counter, taking several deep breaths. Thankfully, the pounding of his heart had eased. The fear that had gushed through his body when he'd feared Mia had drowned, or worse, been torn up by the motor of the boat, had slowly drained away, replaced with the knowledge that he'd almost lost Mia tonight. The notion left him shaky.

His supposedly good idea of putting distance between them had ended up putting her in harm's way. What was the matter with him? He needed to do a better job protecting her. However, he didn't think there was anything he could do to protect his heart. There was no question he'd fallen in love with her. But what was he going to do about it?

Restless energy had him pushing away from the counter. He forced himself to concentrate on the act of ladling the soup into two bowls and buttering the bread, and then put their meal on the kitchen table.

He wouldn't think about the inconvenient and very unprofessional attachment he was developing for Mia. Not tonight. Not until the threat to her was over. Then he would have to figure out how to proceed.

He wouldn't risk the kind of hurt he had experienced when Kelsey broke off their engagement. So he'd need to discover how to extract himself from Mia.

Only he didn't think that was going to be possible without damaging his heart. But it had to be done.

For now, he had to focus on his next steps. And that was looking deeper into Ron Davies. If the man was guilty of harming Mia—in any way— he was going to pay.

After a restless night reliving, again and again, the moment the large silver pontoon had plowed over the top of Mia's boat, Nelson was glad for the caffeine jolt of Mia's delicious coffee. He needed it to stay focused as he drove them to the marina. Mia would not let him leave the house without her, much to his irritation. He understood. She had a stake in learning if Ron Davies was the one who'd been trying to kill her. And Nelson had been torn between keeping her close or leaving her at the house unprotected. When it came down to it, he knew he needed to keep her within arm's reach. Between him and Diesel, they would protect her. No more distance. He'd learned his lesson on the lake.

After discovering more about Ron from his call with Russ, Nelson had a better idea who he was dealing with. Ron had a business degree from the state college and had taken out a loan to start his rental equipment business. He'd been married for a short time but was now divorced and living in a one-bedroom apartment in Dillon. From all accounts, the man was just like any other average guy trying to find his way. Except, maybe, for a potential murderous streak.

Nelson and Mia found Ron behind the counter of his state-of-the-art equipment rental shop. At least four times as large as Mia's, with nearly as many racks for equipment that were currently empty because they'd all been rented. And by the number of people coming and going, there was no doubt his business was booming.

He had a monopoly on the lake at the moment as long as Jem's Rentals was out of commission. Motive for murder?

THIRTEEN

Nelson noticed Ron had his arm in a sling. Nelson's fingers itched to arrest the man. But he had to proceed with caution, not jump the gun without proper procedure.

Ron frowned when he caught sight of them. He wore water-resistant pants and a long-sleeve polo-style shirt with his company logo on the breast pocket. He called to one of his assistants, urging the employee near.

After whispering in the young man's ear, Ron came out from behind the cash register, his chest popped out a bit and his chin jutted upward. "I told you if you had any more questions to contact my lawyer."

"How did you hurt your shoulder?" Nelson asked, ignoring Ron's statement and watching the man closely.

Ron glanced at his shoulder and back at Nelson with a frown. "Who says it's my shoulder? What does it matter to you?"

"It matters." Nelson stared him down. Beside him, Nelson sensed Mia's agitation, but he'd made her promise to let him do the talking. And so far, she was keeping her word. He was grateful for however long she managed to stay quiet.

"I wrenched it playing a game of pickup basketball," Ron ground out. "Again, if you have anything else you need to say to me, go through my lawyer."

"I could arrest you now," Nelson told him.

Ron's eyes widened and his chin dipped. "On what grounds?"

"Attempted murder," Nelson replied.

Ron's mouth pressed into a thin line. "You have nothing on me. I didn't shoot up her cabin."

"But you tried to—" Mia started and stopped when her gaze met Nelson's.

Nelson raised his eyebrows and gave her a pointed look she must've interpreted correctly, because she made a zipper gesture across her mouth.

With a nod, Nelson turned back to Ron. "You rent out pontoon boats, correct?"

Ron shrugged, then winced when the movement clearly hurt his shoulder. "Yes, I do. What does that have to do with anything?"

"We'll get to that," Nelson said. "Where were you day before yesterday, in the morning?"

"Playing a game of pickup basketball," Ron said. "Where I injured myself."

"I'll need to verify your alibi. Where'd you play ball?"

Ron rolled his eyes. "At the community rec center. You can ask Jennifer at the front desk. She'll vouch for me. Why are you asking me these questions?"

"Where were you yesterday afternoon?" Though Nelson didn't think the man he'd seen driving the pontoon boat had sported a sling.

"Here." Ron turned his gaze to Mia. "What have you gotten yourself into now?"

It took all of Nelson's self-possession not to grab the man by the throat. "Someone in one of your pontoon boats rammed into her kayak and tried to kill her."

Ron's gaze bounced between them, and he held up his good hand. "Wasn't me."

"Then I want to see all the records of who rented pontoon boats yesterday afternoon," Nelson said.

A smirk crossed Ron's face. "When you have a court order or warrant or whatever it is called, then I can show you my records. My clients' privacy is guaranteed."

Mia made a distressed noise in her throat, and a growl emanated from Diesel. Ron took a step back.

Keeping his voice as calm as he could, Nelson replied, "I'll be back with a warrant for your records. They better not be altered."

"I have nothing to hide," Ron told them. "But I do have a business to run. And as you can see, it's booming."

The jab had Mia stepping forward, her bandaged hands coming up as if she wanted to pop Ron in the nose. Nelson didn't blame her. The man was insufferable. Obnoxious and arrogant beyond reason. And clearly hiding something.

Without another word, Nelson urged Mia and Diesel out of the rental shop before he gave in to the temptation to throttle Ron Davies. The way he rubbed his success in Mia's face was enough to make Nelson's blood boil.

As soon as they were outside, Mia said, "Can you believe his gall? I gave him the injury to his shoulder when I hit him with the oar!"

"You might be right." Nelson hoped so. Then he could arrest the jerk.

As they walked to his vehicle, Nelson pulled out his phone and called Jodie at headquarters, asking if she'd look into Ron's claim of a pickup basketball game and his injury, and requesting her to start the ball rolling on a warrant for the rental equipment records.

Working to lower his blood pressure with breathing exercises, he drove them back to Mia's cabin and parked. He popped open the back compartment remotely for Diesel to hop out. The dog ran toward the woods, then halted, standing stock-still.

Frowning at his partner's behavior, Nelson climbed out of the vehicle and came around to open Mia's door. He watched as Diesel lifted his nose and cocked his head. Diesel spun around to face the cabin.

Uneased landed like a stone in a pool inside Nelson's stomach. "Stay here," he said to Mia. "Something has Diesel alerting."

"Be careful," Mia said, her voice filled with fear.

Nelson approached Diesel and the dog glanced at him and cautiously approached the cabin, sniffing his way up the stairs to the porch. He stopped in front of the door and pawed the ground. Definitely alerting.

Nelson joined Diesel on the porch. "You smell something?"

Moving closer to inspect the door, Diesel growled a warning just as a series of pops jolted through the quiet forest. Recognizing the sound of an ignition device, Nelson grabbed Diesel by the caller and jumped back. Scooping the dog up in his arms, he dove off the porch just as the front of the cabin burst into flames.

Heart thundering in his chest, Nelson and Diesel raced away from the fire now engulfing Mia's cabin. Stopping near his SUV, he set his partner on his feet, took out his phone and dialed 911. After identifying himself, he said, "Hurry. We need the fire department." He gave the dispatcher the address, then hung up.

Mia stood beside him, her shocked gaze taking in the destruction of her home. "What just happened?"

"There was a timer that went off as we were standing there. It ignited the flames."

"Just like the dock fire," she said in a shaky voice. "We have to do something! My life is inside that cabin."

Nelson wasn't sure there was much to be done, but he still grabbed the small fire extinguisher he kept in one of his utility boxes inside the SUV.

It wasn't much, but at least he could try to minimize the damage. He stood as close as he could get without being burned and sprayed the white foam on the flames curling from the door and window. The fire burned strong and ate up the wooden cabin like tinder, fast and easily.

The whine of a siren filled the air. Soon the fire department was there, relieving him and putting out the flames. Nelson stepped out of the way and moved to stand beside Mia. He put an arm around her waist and she leaned into him. Tears streaked her face, and his heart squeezed tight. She shouldn't have to suffer these losses.

"What happened this time?" the fire chief asked, coming to stand with them, watching the fire crew.

Holding onto his anger so he didn't unleash it on the man, Nelson explained. "There was some sort of timer that set off the ignition. I'm sure you'll find the same sort of device that started the fire that burned Mia's dock."

The fire chief grunted. "We'll see. Our investigation of the dock fire shows the accelerant used was butane." His gaze raked over Mia, then settled back on Nelson before the chief turned and walked away to confer with his men.

"He thinks I torched my own dock and house," Mia stated quietly.

"We know the truth," he told her. "We'll find the culprit and put a stop to this." He sent up a prayer that he could make good on his promise.

Diesel strained at his lead. Nelson let him off leash and the dog raced into the woods. He barked, ran back toward them and then turned and disappeared amongst the trees again. Nelson and Mia followed to where the dog sat just inside the tree line. Three empty butane canisters lay discarded in the brush. There was no doubt in Nelson's mind that whoever did this was somehow connected to the warehouse fire. But it couldn't have been Ron Davies. They'd left him at his rental shop. But he could have set it up earlier. But when? Was he working with someone?

Once the fire was out and the firefighters had packed up, the fire chief warned Nelson not to go near the structure until he said it was okay.

Watching the fire truck drive away, Nelson said to Mia, "Obviously, you can't stay here. You'll come with me to Denver. My bungalow's small, but safe."

"I can go to a hotel," she said, her voice dejected.

He was having none of that. "I'm not letting you out of my sight."

She stared at him for a moment. "Can I get anything from the house?"

"Not until the fire investigation is concluded and it's safe," he told her. "It should only be a day or two. Then we can come back and see what can be salvaged."

The slam of a vehicle door had Nelson tensing.

Xander Beckman loped toward them. "Mia! Are you okay?"

"Yes. Just my house is destroyed." She wrapped her arms around her middle.

Flicking a glance at the burned structure, Xander said, "You can come stay with me. I've got plenty of room."

Dislike cramped Nelson's gut. He was about to

tell the other man where he could take his offer, when Mia said, "I appreciate your concern, Xander. I really do. But I'm going to Denver."

Xander's blue eyes shifted toward Nelson and there was no mistaking the malice in the man's expression. Clearly, Xander didn't like having competition for Mia's attention, just as Nelson has supposed.

Xander turned back to Mia, disappointment written on his face. "Suit yourself. But you know how to find me."

He stomped back through the mud and water left by the firefighters' efforts to his silver truck and drove away. Something about the truck poked at Nelson as it had the first time Xander had shown up. But he couldn't say why. Putting the man out of his mind, Nelson said, "There's not much we can do here."

Mia sighed. "I'm glad all of the evidence I collected is now with your forensic lab. Or it would be up in flames."

Nelson turned back to look at the burnt-out shell of the cabin. Was that the arsonist's intent?

Something to consider.

"We can stop at a store and get you some clothes," Nelson told her as he helped her into the SUV.

She grimaced. "I don't really have extra funds to buy a whole new wardrobe."

"We'll figure that out," he told her. "Let me take care of the details."

From the consternation on her face and the way she was biting her lip, he could tell she was struggling with the idea. As independent and self-reliant as she was, it would be hard for her to accept this level of help. He would do everything he could to ease her into acceptance.

Mia sat on the back porch of Nelson's home and sipped the coffee he had given her. When he'd said he had a small bungalow, he'd minimized exactly where he lived or the beauty of his surroundings.

His home was a midcentury beauty at the end of a cul-de-sac, on top of a rise that looked out at the Denver skyline and the Rockies beyond. Original woodwork gave the inside character while the updated granite counters and luxury stone tile flooring made the place spectacular. Though the space was sparsely furnished. And the outside landscaping showed the love and care Nelson had put into his property. Diesel had a nice square yard to roam with grass and flowering bushes.

This moment of respite, sitting next to Nelson while enjoying the morning, filled Mia with a kind of restless yearning she didn't understand. The events of yesterday had passed in a haze—

her house going up in flames and the exchange with Xander that seemed odd, and then driving to Denver where Nelson had stopped at a department store. It had been hard for her to allow him to buy her a week's worth of clothes and toiletries.

How had she come to this point where she had to rely on this man?

She took a sip of her coffee and glanced over the rim at him. He held his mug between his big capable hands, his gaze staring out at the vista. She still didn't understand why he was helping her. She didn't understand why she was permitting it. There was something about him, something that called to her deep inside. Was it love? She didn't really know. She could fancy herself falling in love with him, but what did she know of the emotion? She'd never been in love. She only knew that she didn't deserve any sort of happiness while Lindsey was still incarcerated.

"I made an appointment for a video call with Lindsey for later this morning," she told him.

"She's out of isolation?"

"I hope so. I'll know when I go to initiate the call," she said. "I was thinking it might be a good way to introduce you."

"Good idea. I'm sure she has a hard time trusting law enforcement at this point."

While the reminder of what Lindsey had gone

through poked at the raw spot inside Mia, Nelson's approval warmed her from the inside.

Almost simultaneously, the sound of two distinct cell phones ringing reached them. They glanced at each other and burst into laughter. It felt good to laugh, felt good to release some of the tension of the past week.

They both set their coffee mugs on the little round table between their wicker chairs and headed inside the house, going separate ways. He headed to the kitchen where he'd left his cell phone charging. She went down the hall to his bedroom, where she'd slept the night before while he'd taken the couch. She knew this arrangement wouldn't last. At some point she'd have to figure out her life, but for now she was safe. Despite the fact that somebody wanted her dead.

As much as she desired to ignore the danger and ignore that she was frightened down to her toes, she knew staying put for the time being was the best course of action. She snatched her cell phone from where she'd plugged it into the wall socket. The number for the Dillon Fire Department showed up on the screen.

"Hello?" she answered.

"Mia?" a deep voice queried.

Recognizing the fire chief's voice, she said, "Yes, Chief." A flutter of hope pounded against her rib cage. "Can I get into my house? Was anything saved from the fire?"

"You can get into the house," the chief told her. "As for what might be salvageable, only you can determine that. Much of the front part of the house is charred. You might find some things upstairs worth keeping."

She prayed the pictures that she had of Jem were intact.

"Thank you, Chief," she said. "I will be there today to see what I can save."

"Just let me know when you're headed over. I'll meet you there," the chief said.

Mia tucked in her chin with surprise. "Why?"

"Mia, this town has not given you a fair shake."

She nearly fell over from shock. Apparently, he realized someone was really after her and now regretted how he'd reacted to the dock fire.

The chief cleared his throat. "I owe it to your parents and Jem to make sure that you're safe when you're inside the wreckage of your home."

Both of his statements burrowed in deep. He was right. The town had vilified her from the day she'd been arrested. And they continued to do so. She wasn't sure the chief owed her parents anything, but Jem had been a vital part of the community. "Thank you, Chief."

She hung up and tucked her phone into her

backpack-style purse. Hopefully, Nelson would be able to drive her home.

"What do you have for me, Russ?" Nelson said into the phone. Mia had retreated to the bedroom, leaving him privacy to talk to Russ.

It amazed Nelson how much he liked having Mia in his home. She was a force to be reckoned with, a mighty spirit packed within a petite form, exuding so much energy and grace. He'd expected her to fall apart after watching her cabin burn, but she'd held it together. There'd been tears of sadness but not of self-pity. The woman was resilient and courageous. His admiration and respect for her grew with each passing day that he spent with her. As well as the love growing within his heart. A love he wasn't sure what to do about.

"I'm here with Jodie," Russ told him, drawing his attention back to the call.

Though he could only guess why both of them were on the call, he braced as trepidation gnawed at his gut. "Okay."

"Do you know how much Mia Turner has researched arson and how to get away with the crime?" Russ asked.

A shiver of unease slithered down Nelson's back. He forcefully ignored it. "I'm sure she's trying to figure out how the person who set the warehouse party fire framed her and Lindsey."

"About that," Jodie said. "I talked to the district attorney. He's convinced that Lindsey and Mia orchestrated the fire. He wasn't happy with the decision of the jury not to convict Mia. The jury decided the evidence was circumstantial."

Frustration bubbled in his blood. "Of course, he's not happy. He wanted a two-for-one conviction. But the jury couldn't get to the decision that Mia was guilty because she wasn't." He didn't need any proof in addition to knowing Mia. "Do you have anything new for me?"

Jodie spoke. "Ron Davies's alibi of a pickup basketball game checks out. He did tweak his shoulder during play."

Nelson grunted his frustration.

"I scoured through Lindsey's computer," Russ interjected, "searching for any sort of malware, virus, hacking or spoofing that would hide the IP address of an outside computer. I found nothing that would support Mia's supposition that somebody other than Lindsey Gates wrote that confession note."

Dread cramped Nelson's chest. Disappointment descended on his shoulders. "None at all? Don't you find that suspicious?"

"Normally, I would," Russ told him. "But this computer had been brand-new when it was confiscated as evidence. There was very little on it.

The only logical conclusion is that Lindsey Gates wrote the confession note on the computer."

Nelson scrubbed his free hand over his jaw. "To what purpose?"

"You're not going to like this," Jodie said.

"Tell me."

"According to Mrs. Gates, Lindsey was suicidal back then. The DA thinks she'd written that note intending to die in the fire she allegedly set but got cold feet at the last moment and bailed."

Why hadn't Mia mentioned this? Had Mia and Lindsey had a suicide pact? No. Absolutely not. Mia was too full of life, too determined and stubborn to ever allow herself to get so low that she'd contemplate ending her life. "But she and Mia came together." Had Lindsey wanted to hurt her friend, as well?

"I don't know what to tell you other than the facts and forensics support the conviction," Russ stated.

"What about the butane canisters in the back of Lindsey's trunk? There was no evidence in the report I read saying that she had bought, stolen or in any other way obtained the butane canisters," Nelson pointed out.

"But her fingerprints were found on a piece of scrap from the exploded butane canister," Jodie reminded him.

"True, but not on the canisters in her trunk."

Nelson understood Mia's frustration. This case had holes and contradictions throughout it. It was unsurprising Mia was obsessed with trying to figure the truth out. The case was a puzzle where the pieces didn't fit together.

FOURTEEN

"The bottom line is," Jodie said into the phone, "the DA is not going to reopen this case."

Impotent frustration reared within Nelson. Of course the district attorney wouldn't want to re-investigate something he'd already closed. To do so would show him in a bad light. But wasn't justice worth more than the man's embarrassment?

"The sergeant wants you back at headquarters," Jodie stated.

Shaking his head, Nelson said, "Mia is still in danger." He wasn't going to give up on her, leaving her unprotected. He told them about the fire purposely set at her cabin. Someone was very determined to hurt her.

"That's scary. You'll need to talk to Tyson," Jodie said. "He's in a meeting at the moment with Michael Bridges. He'd like you to come in."

Nelson didn't envy his boss. Special Agent in Charge Michael Bridges could be intense in the best of circumstances; Nelson could only imagine how the SAC was taking the training incident.

"I'll be in as soon as I can," Nelson told Jodie and hung up.

He stood there for a long moment, lost in contemplation. He'd take Mia with him to headquarters and convince his boss not to pull him off Mia's case. But what had him tied in knots was how was he going to tell Mia the case against her friend was solid.

Mia's assertion that Lindsey was framed rang in his head.

Could there be a slim possibility whoever framed Lindsey had done such a thorough job as to make Lindsey appear guilty?

He understood Mia really wanted to believe her friend innocent when she might not be. But it was time for Mia to move on with her life. A life that wouldn't include him.

Mia found Nelson staring out the kitchen window, his cell phone still gripped in his big hand. "Nelson?"

He turned, the grim expression on his handsome face halting her steps. Anxiety unfurled within her. "What is it?"

"That was Russ and Jodie."

"Both of them?"

"Yes," he said. "It doesn't look good. In fact, it's not good."

She steeled herself against what he was going to tell her. "What are you talking about? Has something happened to Lindsey?"

"This does have to do with Lindsey, but she's fine as far as I know."

Mia let out a relieved breath. "Then just spit it out." She couldn't keep the irritation out of her tone. He didn't normally hedge. And it made her uneasy.

"Russ and his team have looked through all of the evidence the DA presented at trial and everything you've gathered through your investigation. They can't find any evidence to support your theory that Lindsey was framed."

For a moment, Mia stared at him, her brain trying to make sense of what he was saying. "What about her computer?"

"It was new and had no malware or viruses and had not been hacked or spoofed."

Everything inside Mia rebelled. "Lindsey did not write that note." Mia's voice rose with the force of her exasperation. "Someone else must have gained access to her computer."

"Who? And when?"

She wanted to scream. "I don't know."

"Did you know that Lindsey's mother claimed she was suicidal?"

Mia gnashed her teeth together. She waved a hand in the air, swatting away the notion as she would a fly. If only she could swat away Mrs. Gates's claim as easily. "Mrs. Gates did not know her daughter. I did. She was not suicidal."

His expression softened in obvious sympathy. "I'm just telling you what we know. The case against Lindsey is solid."

Disappointment and resignation threatened to drown her. She fought to stay afloat. Echoes of all the times her parents, Jem and Xander had said Lindsey was guilty swashed over her like the wake of a speedboat. The whole town had cheered the day Lindsey had gone to prison, certain of her guilt and refusing to listen to Mia's protests. "You're just like everyone else. You don't believe me."

She'd let herself trust him. Trust that he'd see beyond the obvious and help her discover the truth. That he'd trust *her*. A huge mistake. She couldn't count on him or anyone else to help her prove Lindsey's innocence. Mia lost the fight against her disappointment and sank deep. Her lungs were mired in despair.

Without another word, she retreated back to the bedroom and arranged for a rideshare. She was going home. At least to what was left of it. She fought back tears as she gathered the meager belongings she now possessed, thanks to Nelson, back into the shopping bags.

Ten minutes later, she heard a honk outside. Taking the bags in hand, she left the bedroom and headed for the front door.

"Where do you think you're going?" Nelson asked from the living room.

"Home," she said, her throat tight from unshed tears. "The fire chief called to say I could get into the cabin and try to see what I could manage to save."

Concern darkened Nelson's gaze. "And then?"

"Frankly, Nelson, it's none of your business." She opened the door and stepped out into the morning sunshine.

He followed her. "It is my business. You're still in danger. I can't let you go off alone."

"You can't keep me here," she said, then winced at the blatant reflection of the turmoil going on inside of her. She wanted him to go with her, but she wouldn't ask. She wanted to be more than a job to him. She wanted him to care enough to put aside his doubts and support her investigation. But wanting anything from anyone only ever led to disappointment.

"Please, don't go." His hand settled heavily on her shoulder.

"I have to." She shrugged him off and hurried to the minivan waiting at the curb.

"Mia!"

Ignoring Nelson's call, she climbed inside the rideshare and shut the door. "Can you take me to the closest car rental agency?"

"Sure thing," the young man behind the wheel said.

As they drove through Nelson's neighborhood, Mia caught a glimpse of a silver truck parked in front of a house a block away from Nelson's. Just like Xander's truck. But his vehicle wouldn't be parked somewhere in the middle of a Denver suburb, so far from Dillon. He was no doubt off fishing, hiking or camping. Or doing whatever it was he did when not traveling for his sales job.

Why wasn't she attracted to Xander? He'd been such a good friend and confidant over the years. They had fun together and she enjoyed hanging out with him, but she didn't harbor romantic affection for him.

Not like the way she held Nelson close to her heart.

The look of utter astonishment on his face as she'd walked out of his house was burned into her mind. Should he really be surprised? She'd told him often enough she didn't need him, didn't want him in her life. Admittedly false statements born out of a need to protect herself. But Nelson didn't know that. Still, he'd treated her with kindness, compassion and protectiveness.

Guilt and regret tugged at her heart. She shouldn't have reacted so poorly and walked out. Although he'd told her the case behind Lindsey's conviction was concrete, his actions had been supportive. He didn't deserve Mia's anger. It wasn't his fault that whoever had framed Lindsey, and tried to frame Mia, for the warehouse fire had done a thorough job.

When she reached the car rental agency, she paid the rideshare driver and hurried to the little kiosk. She requested whatever car was available. Within twenty minutes, she was on her way back to Dillon. She called the chief to let him know and he promised to meet her at her cabin, telling her not to enter without him. After chewing her lip raw, she called Nelson's cell but got voice mail. She hung up without leaving a message. Then decided to send him a text.

Hi Nelson, I need to apologize for my behavior this morning. I hope you'll forgive me, she typed into the phone and hit Send. Needing to tell him her plan, she typed, I'm going to meet the fire chief at the cabin, grab some things and then head back to your house. I hope that's okay. She hit Send again and shook her head. He'd probably think she was wishy-washy.

Once she arrived back at her cabin in Dillon, her heart broke to see the damage done to the front of the house by the fire. Since the fire chief hadn't arrived yet, she walked around to the back porch, discovering it had fared better. Her deck chairs had been pulled away from the structure and set aside.

A ding on her phone reminded her of the video call she'd set up with Lindsey. She'd been so flustered by what Nelson had said, she'd forgotten the video call had been scheduled for right now. She grabbed a chair and took a seat. Though Mia had hoped Nelson would be with her when she had this call, it couldn't be helped. Once a video call reservation was made, she had to honor it or lose it.

Whether by video or in person, their conversations were monitored because law enforcement was always listening, hoping they would say something incriminating. But there wasn't anything nefarious about their visits.

Sending up a prayer that Lindsey would be available, Mia got out her phone and opened the app that would allow her to make the video call. A cool breeze, tainted with the acrid smell of burnt cabin, blew across the back of Mia's neck as she waited for the connection to go through. The sun shone bright overhead and she turned the deck chair to face the back of the house to keep the sun's reflection off her smartphone so she could see the image on the screen.

Her mind replayed Nelson's comment that the

case against Lindsey was solid. That she'd supposedly been suicidal. Mia had never seen anything to hint at depression in Lindsey. Not even when things were so bad at home and she'd come to Mia's to stay, much to Mia's parents' dismay. They had never approved of Lindsey but they'd tolerated her, until the fire.

After a long moment of waiting, suddenly, Lindsey's face filled the small screen of Mia's phone. Mia knew that on Lindsey's end she was being viewed on a computer used for video conferencing set up in the common room of the prison. Mia's heart squeezed tight. Lindsey's face was swollen and black and blue from her fight that had landed her in isolation.

Lindsey gasped. "Mia, what happened to you?"

Mia touched her face, having forgotten her own bruises. "Car accident."

Only, not an accident. But she didn't want to worry her friend.

A couple of women, all wearing the same bright yellow T-shirt and green pants, crowded around Lindsey, trying to see Mia.

"Whoa, she don't look so good," one woman leaning over Lindsey's shoulder commented.

Lindsey shooed the woman away. But several stayed in the background, hovering. It wasn't unusual for the other inmates to want to see something from the outside. Mia couldn't imagine the torment of being locked away inside the dank, gray walls.

"I'm glad to see you," Mia told her friend. "We were going to come earlier this week to visit but you were in isolation. What happened?"

"Nothing worth talking about." Lindsey's eyebrows rose. "But you said *we*. Do tell."

Mia's face warmed. "It's not what you think. I had someone helping me, but now he's not." Because she'd walked out on him. She really needed to apologize to Nelson in person. To set things right between them. To tell him…she shied away from confessing her feelings for him. She couldn't go there emotionally yet. If ever.

Lindsey worried her lip. "Please tell me you aren't still hanging out with Xander."

Mia tucked in her chin. "What is it with you two? You never liked each other."

Lindsey looked away. When her gaze returned to the screen, she said, "Just be careful, okay?"

Always the same warning. "Why?"

"Just trust me. He and his gang were not good people."

Her statement brought back to mind a question Lindsey had dodged before. "Tell me about your date with Andy Walsh."

Lindsey drew back. She glanced around as if checking to see who would overhear her. "Why are you asking about that? Ancient history."

"Is it? You won't talk about the date, so it seems pretty important."

"I can't."

Mia had a horrible suspicion that whatever had happened had left her friend scarred emotionally. Normally, she wouldn't insist out of respect for her friend's privacy, but desperate for something to help shed new light on the past and the fire, she pressed, "Yes, you can. It's been almost ten years since that date. You said he was a jerk. But why? What happened?"

Lindsey toyed with her hair, indecision written over her battered face. Finally, she said, "They were all there."

Mia hated how the sensation of dread had become so familiar. "What do you mean *they were all there*?"

Lindsey sighed and leaned closer to the screen, lowering her voice. "Andy picked me up and took me to the far side of the lake."

The opposite side of the lake from Jem's Rentals. Mia's heart hammered in her chest. It was a place a lot of the kids went to be alone from the prying eyes of parents and law enforcement.

Lindsey continued, "And Ron, Xander, Kyle and a few others from the football team were there."

Horror and outrage flooded Mia. Awful scenarios played through her mind like the images on a flip board. "Did they hurt you?"

Lindsey bared her teeth. "They tried, but I came prepared." She gave a self-effacing laugh. "I'd brought bear spray with me in my purse, and I sprayed them all. And then I ran."

The air left Mia's lungs in a swoosh of relief. She was glad for her friend's spunk. "Why didn't you tell me? Why didn't you tell the police?"

A sad, resigned look entered Lindsey's eyes. "Who do you think they were going to believe? Me or the stars of the high school football team?"

She had a point. Still, it wasn't right. Or fair. But then again, Mia knew firsthand life wasn't fair. "What did they do in retaliation?"

Lindsey arched a swollen and bruised eyebrow. "You tell me."

Mia's breath stalled. Had this incident been the motive for framing Lindsey for the fire? "Did you tell your lawyer about what happened?"

"I did," she replied. "He said it was irrelevant."

Distressed, Mia wanted to scream at how unjust life could be. Lindsey's lawyer had been court appointed and had had several cases going at once. He'd seemed to consider the case against Lindsey too airtight to bother fighting. If Mia's parents hadn't hired a private criminal attorney, she might be in the jail cell next to Lindsey now.

As succinctly as possible, Mia relayed all that had happened over the past week.

Lindsey's eyes grew round. "That's awful. Are you safe? Who is this Nelson guy?"

"He's with the Rocky Mountain K-9 Unit," Mia told her. "He's really nice and has tried to help. He won't think this information is irrelevant."

"I'm afraid to hope." Lindsey set her chin in her palm. "Tell me more about Nelson. Nice and handsome?"

Nelson's stunning blue eyes and strong shoulders came to mind and Mia smiled. "Yes, handsome." Hearing the wistful tone in her own voice, she was quick to add, "But there's nothing going on." Even though she secretly wished for something to be going on between them.

"Right." Lindsey laughed. "You're blushing."

Making a face, Mia decided to change the subject to the most important topic. "The FBI has your computer, but they can't figure out how the note got onto it."

Sobering, Lindsey sat forward, her voice dropping. "I did not write that letter."

"I know," Mia assured her. "But then who?"

With a sigh filled with exasperation, Lindsey said, "I don't know, but somebody else must have gotten into my bedroom and got onto my computer. That's the only explanation."

They'd gone over this before and always ended

up in the same place. Nowhere. "But there's no way of proving that."

The Gates home had been sold not long after Lindsey went to jail. The new owners had totally taken the house down to the studs and rebuilt. There was no evidence left to support their claim that someone other than Lindsey had broken in to type the confession, and no one had cared about their claims of being framed at the time.

"I'm not going to stop trying to figure this out," Mia promised her.

Lindsey shook her head, frowning. "Mia, you've got to live your own life."

"Not until you can, too."

Lindsey's eyes widened and terror filled her eyes. "Mia, watch out!"

An arm slid around Mia's throat, choking her and knocking the phone from her hand. The device landed on the ground.

Panic swept through Mia like a gale wind. She let out a scream that was silenced by a hand over her mouth. She scratched at the hand and tried to stand, to get away, but her assailant held on tight.

Soon the world faded as the arm around her neck increased the pressure…until there was nothing.

FIFTEEN

Awareness jolted through Mia as her surroundings infiltrated the fog of unconsciousness. The sound of tires rolling on pavement had her eyelids flying open and she tried to gasp but couldn't. Her mouth had been taped shut. Panic clawed through her. She was in the back seat of a truck's crew cab, lying on her side. Xander sat in the driver's seat. Confusion filled her mind. What was going on?

She moved to sit up and realized with horror that her hands were bound together behind her back with duct tape. So were her feet. Had Xander rescued her from the person who'd choked her unconscious? Or had he been the one to grab her from behind at her cabin?

Mia's world began to spiral downward, and darkness threatened at the edges of her vision. He was someone she'd considered as a friend and confidant. Someone she'd trusted. Why was he doing this?

Her mind wouldn't allow herself to contemplate the worst. There had to be a logical explanation. This was Xander.

Desperate, she wanted to yell at him for answers, but could only make ineffectual noises in her throat. Using her elbow and her core muscles, she pushed herself to her hip. There wasn't room between the front passenger seat and the bench seat she lay on for her to put her feet on the floorboard.

She met Xander's gaze in the rearview mirror. She shrank back from the hard expression darkening his blue eyes.

"Lie back down, Mia," he instructed. "I don't want to have to hurt you."

But he already had, by choking her unconscious, binding her hands and feet and taking her to some unknown fate. Rocked to the core, she realized she was seeing the real Xander for the first time. Fear lanced through her, causing her to break out in a cold sweat.

Xander reached behind him with a big hand and pushed her hard so she was down to her side again. She flopped onto the bench seat like a fish on a dock. Her mind whirled.

Think! she commanded herself. At the very least she needed to find out where he was taking her, trussed up as she was.

Despite his threat of harm, she pushed herself

upright again as best she could and looked out the window. They were headed along Highway 70 out of Dillon. But to where? She twisted to look out the back window, hoping to somehow get the attention of the car behind them. Panic tightened its grip when she realized that the other car was too far back for her to do anything besides will it to see her and know she was in trouble. Not likely at all.

She heard Xander engage the turn signal then change course onto a bumpy, unpaved road. Trees dotted the landscape. She shifted to see what lay ahead. An older, ranch-style house came into view.

Recognition hit her. Xander's parents' property. Why was he bringing her here?

He brought the truck to a halt around the back of the house, near a large barn. Without a word, he popped open his door and climbed out.

If she could get in the driver's seat and shut the door, she could lock him out. Only she could hardly move, given her bound hands, feet and the awkward position she'd been forced into.

Through the front windshield, she watched as Xander went to the barn doors, sliding them open. Sunlight glinted off the grill of a semitrailer truck. Her breath caught in her throat. She recognized that truck. Xander had been the one trying to drive Nelson, her and Diesel off the road.

He'd already tried to hurt them. Her blood froze in her veins.

Had Xander been behind all the attacks against her? Had he been the one to shoot at her? Had he set fire to her dock? Tried to run her over with a pontoon? And attempted to burn her house down? Considering she was now tied up in his truck after being choked to unconsciousness, the answer was clear.

Stunned by the revelation, she could only ask herself why he would do all those awful things.

The question reverberated through her brain on a loop that threatened to drive her out of her mind as she struggled against her bonds.

She'd thought they were friends. He'd been the one to offer comfort when she was so distraught after Lindsey's sentencing. He'd written to her often after he left for college. Then, when he'd returned, he'd reclaimed her friendship, making her feel not so alone. He'd been her confidant. She'd trusted him.

Apparently, she had no idea how trust worked. Maybe she was just gullible. Whichever it was, she would not be fooled again.

Xander returned, hopped back behind the wheel and drove the truck inside the barn and parked. Dust motes danced in the beams of the bright noon sunlight streaming through the windows high in the barn walls. Once the engine was off, he climbed out and opened the rear cab door.

She attempted to scoot away from him, but there was nowhere to go. She screamed behind the tape and shook her head.

Xander simply smiled in return. With a laugh that sent chills of terror cascading down her spine, he grabbed her by the shoulders and hauled her out of the truck. Her feet landed on the concrete floor with a thud. Keeping a hold of her shoulders with one arm, Xander placed his other arm beneath her knees and easily scooped her up. She shied away from him, thrashing to get free.

"Stop it!" he commanded in a voice as rough as sandpaper that she'd never heard him use. "I'll drop you and drag you, if you want."

She stilled.

"Good girl," he uttered and stalked out of the barn toward the house, only he didn't go inside but toward a door built into the ground just to the right of the back porch.

A root cellar. Her stomach sank with dismay. He wouldn't put her in there, would he?

He dropped her on the ground so hard the landing jarred through her, making her teeth knock together. She winced beneath the tape over her mouth as pain pounded in her jaw. She used the pain to fuel her anger and determination to escape.

While he worked to undo the lock of the wooden door, she twisted and rolled to her hip. Using her elbows for leverage, she inched way from him as best she could, the dirt and debris digging into her flesh.

She shuddered as Xander barked out another awful laugh. "Where do you think you can go?"

Tears of frustration burned her eyes, but she kept moving. Her gaze intent on the stack of wood beyond the house. And the ax. If she could only get to it…a hysterical bubble of fear nearly choked her. How could she use the ax when her hands were tied behind her back?

Then he was standing in front of her, his booted feet blocking the way. Roughly, he grabbed her and hauled her to her feet, her anklebones grinding together beneath the tight duct tape. With one beefy hand around her biceps, he dragged her forward toward whatever horror awaited her in the cellar's blackness, forcing her to hop on both feet to stay upright.

At the yawning dark mouth of the cellar, terror overcame her and she thrashed, uncaring that she lost her balance. He released his hold and let her drop to the ground. Her backside met the dirt with a resounding crash that agonizingly pulsated up her spine.

Sitting with her knees bent, she desperately looked around, searching for help, but there was none to be found. The grass was overgrown all the way to the forest in the distance. The green paint on the house peeled and curled, making it clear the home hadn't been cared for. Wasn't he supposed to be getting his parents' place ready to sell?

Not that he'd had the opportunity to work on it, what with terrorizing her by shooting at her, burning down her dock and her cabin…

A frightening thought slammed through her. Was he planning to burn this house down with her in it?

"Please!" she cried, though the muffled sound was unintelligible.

He huffed in exasperation, reached down and yanked the duct tape off her mouth. She yelped with pain as bits of skin tore away from her tender lips. Keeping her breathing shallow through the sting of his brutality, she sent up a prayer for protection.

Once the agony around her mouth eased, she said, "Xander, please. I don't understand. I thought we were friends?"

He snorted and spat on the ground. "Friends." He shook his head. "You have no idea. You are oblivious. Always have been."

"Then enlighten me," she said. "Tell me why you're doing this."

"Because I have had a crush on you since

high school," he said. "But you just wanted to be friends. When I kissed you, you laughed at me."

Mind reeling with surprise, she ignored his declaration of affection and said, "I was seventeen and had never been kissed. I reacted like a girl does, by giggling." Outrage that he would blame his current behavior on something that happened over ten years ago replaced her surprise and had her tone sharpening. "You laughed, too, and said you were only joking. How was I supposed to know you had feelings for me?"

He squatted down to her eye level and reached out to run his knuckle down her cheek.

Instinctively, she pulled back.

Grabbing her chin, Xander's fingers bruised the already tender flesh. "See. I've tried so many times to show you how much I cared."

She couldn't deny there had been hints that had made her wonder, but he hadn't done anything to make his intentions known. She'd never dreamt he harbored ill will toward her because she wasn't reciprocating romantic love.

He stood again, towering over her. "In high school, Lindsey was always getting in the way. I thought for sure when she went to jail, you'd turn to me and realize I was the only one you needed. But you didn't."

"I did, too." She stared at this man whom she apparently never really knew. Her panic returned, a slow, growing burn behind her breastbone. "You were the only one there for me besides Jem. I didn't realize the depth of what you felt. You never said anything."

"I shouldn't have to say it," he roared. "You should have known."

"I'm not a mind reader." Did he honestly believe what he was saying? She couldn't fathom the arrogance. Or was it more a lack of confidence that had kept him silent about his feelings? But his reasons didn't matter. Nothing justified what he was doing to her. "You left after the trial, so whatever you felt couldn't have been too deep."

His face twisted with rage. "I left because I had to accept you were never going to see me as anything more than a friend."

Her mouth dried in the face of his anger. "I valued our friendship."

"Not enough to stop digging where you don't belong," he spat.

Digging? Understanding dawned along a deep-seated apprehension. "You mean my investigation into the warehouse fire?" Why wouldn't he want her to discover the truth? "All the attempts on my life were *you* trying to stop me from investigating?" The horror of his actions swept over her like a gale wind off the lake, leaving her icy cold.

"I knew it was only a matter of time before either one of the idiots talked or you figured out what I'd done," he said. "I want to get on with my life and not have to keep waiting for the shoe to drop."

Stunned, she tried to put the pieces of this strange puzzle together. Memories of that night played through her head. The four football stars coming in together. Xander coming over to joke with her, then wandering off with his buddies. Kyle Long attempting to coax Mia to the dance floor. Lindsey's worried expression as Mia gave in and agreed, letting Kyle lead her away. Mia couldn't place Xander until later, when he carried Seaver out of the smoke-filled warehouse. "You started the warehouse fire? Why?"

Xander ran a hand through his hair. "It doesn't matter why."

"But it does," she said. "Lindsey's in jail because of you."

Impotent anger raged within her chest, making her skin hot. She tested the tape around her wrists and ankles but there was no way she could get loose with him standing over her like some ghastly specter.

"Lindsey discovered my crush on you," he said. "She saw the kiss and warned me off. Telling me you were too good for the likes of me. Ha!" He laughed, sounding truly unhinged. "I thought if she were injured and I was there to support you, you'd realize you loved me."

Raising her eyebrows at his flawed logic, she said, "So you started the fire to make me fall in love with you?"

"Yes." He smiled wistfully. "It would have worked. I just know it." His expression darkened. "But then, she walked away to go outside. Before I could get to her, Seaver started yelling at me, then the fire really took off. I didn't expect such big flames or the way the pallet went up so quickly." Xander made a face. "That scrawny nerd. He shouldn't have gotten in the way."

"Gotten in the way?" A sick horror sank in her gut. "Seaver witnessed you start the fire?"

"Yeah, and he would have squealed on me. I couldn't let him do that."

Heart aching for the young boy, she shook her head. "You killed him, not the smoke."

Xander shrugged. "No, the smoke killed him. I just wouldn't let him leave until it did."

She closed her eyes on tears of sorrow and anger and horror. She opened her eyes to stare at the monster before her. "All this time, everyone considered you a hero."

He grinned. "It's the best feeling in the world." He reached down and grasped her arm, hauling her back to the opening of the root cellar.

"No. No, please." She struggled as best she could to break away from his hold. "You don't have to kill me. I'll stop investigating. I'll leave it alone and never tell anyone what you've told me."

"If only it were that simple," he said. "No, you had to bring your boyfriend into the investigation."

Her stomach dropped. A fresh wave of terror tore through her. "Nelson doesn't know anything. You leave him alone."

Xander held her over the dark abyss. "Sorry. He's got to go, too." He pushed her inside.

She rolled down three stairs, the sharp edges battering her body, until she landed in a heap on the dirt floor. The musty odor of disuse and rotted vegetables turned her stomach. She gagged, barely able to keep her stomach from revolting.

"Xander, don't do this!" she screamed and tried to right herself.

He slammed the door shut. Only this wasn't like a normal root cellar; this was a crawlspace that had been converted to a root cellar. She blinked, her eyes adjusting to the little slits of light coming through the cracks in the wood. She could make out the crude shelves jammed into the walls with ancient canning jars filled with murky, indistinguishable contents.

Tears cascaded down her cheeks and she sobbed. She had to escape and warn Nelson. But how?

"Please, Lord, save Nelson."

* * *

Nelson drove toward Dillon, anxiety curling through his system. Traffic was heavy, slowing his progress and building his frustration. Mia hadn't answered his texts or his phone calls. He'd known she was upset, and he understood she needed some distance, but taking off like that left her unprotected and exposed. That didn't sit well with him.

Instead of going to headquarters, he was going to find Mia. Best to let his boss know sooner rather than later. He placed a call to Tyson via the Bluetooth in the SUV.

"I was expecting you here," Tyson said as soon as he came on the line.

"Sorry." Nelson winced. "Jodie did say you wanted me back there, but I can't right now. Mia has taken off on her own. She's headed back to her cabin. I can't shake this deep sense that something's wrong."

Nor could he shake her accusation that he was like everyone else, unwilling to believe her. He accepted that she believed Lindsey was innocent without any proof other than her loyalty. And Nelson decided that was enough. He'd support her no matter what.

"You've fallen for her," Tyson stated rather than asked.

Nelson swallowed as his mouth dried. To have his emotions pointed out was uncomfortable. But there was no denying it. Love and admiration for Mia filled him. "Yes, I have. But I don't know that a relationship with her will ever happen. She's so focused on proving her friend's innocence she doesn't have room for anything else in her life."

"Did she say as much?"

"No," Nelson admitted. "But I do know she won't stop pushing to free her friend. I'm afraid the person trying to harm her won't stop, either."

"Then find her and bring her here," Tyson said. "We'll keep her safe."

Grateful to be part of a team that was more like family than just a group of coworkers, Nelson said, "Thank you. I appreciate your understanding."

"I have to pull Russ and his team from the warehouse fire case. We have other cases needing attention and we still haven't made any progress on the car fire. Lucas has been visiting with Kate Montgomery, but she remains unconscious. There have been no reports of a missing infant."

"It's strange that no one has reported a missing baby. I wish there was more we could do," Nelson said. He and Diesel had done what they could. He didn't like the fact that they were no closer to solving the car fire case.

"We all know that some cases take longer than others. We will pray for a breakthrough," Tyson said.

"Amen to that." Another bond they shared was their faith. "Any news regarding what happened at the training session?"

Tyson made a growling noise that Nelson recognized as frustration. "I've got Special Agent in Charge Michael Bridges breathing down my neck, but he also has his hands full with Congresswoman Clark's murder. I'm working on what happened during the training exercise."

Nelson grimaced. He wouldn't want to be in his boss's shoes right now. But he had no doubt Tyson would leave no stone unturned until he solved that mystery. "How's Shadow?"

"He'll recover. He and Ben are in Wyoming while Shadow recuperates," Tyson said. "Keep me updated on the situation there regarding Mia."

"Yes, I will." Nelson clicked off and concentrated on getting to Mia. Keeping an eye on the rearview mirror as he drove, to avoid another incident like the one with the semitrailer truck, he was thankful Tyson had agreed to let him see this through. He didn't want to be put in the untenable position of having to choose between the team and the woman he was falling for.

As soon as Nelson turned into the driveway, Mia's cabin came into view. The covered front porch had collapsed, leaving a jumbled mess of charred wood. The whole front side had borne the brunt of the damage.

He noted the rental car parked out front. He should have known she'd be resourceful and rent a car. He breathed a sigh of relief that she was here. But wasn't the fire chief supposed to meet her? Where was he?

SIXTEEN

Nelson climbed out of the SUV. The lingering taint of wet, burnt wood hung heavy in the air. He opened Diesel's compartment. Being the well-trained arson detecting dog that he was, Diesel started for the ignition point at the front of the cabin, but Nelson gave a sharp whistle to call him back.

"Mia!" Nelson called out. Had she gone inside the house? If so, she had to go around back because there was no way to enter from the front. He started in that direction just as an official Dillon Fire Department pickup truck rolled up behind Mia's rental car.

The fire chief, Stan Clemens, got out of his rig, extending his hand to Nelson. "Officer Rivers, it's good to see you again."

Nelson shook the offered hand. "Have you seen Mia or heard from her?"

Stan frowned. "She was supposed to meet me here. I assumed she was with you."

"She's not." He pointed to the rental car. "I believe that's hers."

Concern darkened the chief's expression. He eyed the house. "I told her not to go in without me."

Nelson stalked toward the back of the cabin, Stan falling into step with him. Diesel ran ahead. Rounding the corner of the structure, they found Diesel sniffing a lone, toppled chair facing the house. Had Mia been here? Where was she now? Unease and dread cramped his stomach.

Stan inspected the back door. "Still locked. Could she be down at the rental shed?"

"Maybe," Nelson said as he stared at the ground. He pointed to the grooves in the dirt. "Do those look like drag marks to you?" Nelson hoped not, hoped his imagination was getting the better of him.

The fire chief examined the ground. "They do. We better ring the Dillon police chief," Clemens stated. "Whoever set her cabin on fire might have her."

Or she could have called Xander and asked him to pick her up, which seemed unlikely since she had a rental car. Why wasn't she answering his texts or calls? Distressed that something might have happened to her, Nelson asked, "Any leads on *who* set the fire?"

Stan shook his head. "No. But you were right,

the same timing device was used both on the dock and the cabin. We've sent all the evidence to your FBI crime lab. They should have it soon."

Nelson was thankful for that. He was sure Russ and his team would be able to discover anything of use. It would be just a matter of time. But time may not be on their side.

"I have to find her." A sense of urgency pushed Nelson.

"I'll alert the police chief," Clemens promised as he climbed back into his rig. "I'll make sure he has patrol keep an eye out for her."

"Thank you." Nelson was glad not to have to deal with the Dillon police chief again. Finding Mia was the priority. After putting Diesel back in his compartment, he climbed into the driver's seat and drummed his fingers on the steering wheel.

Where could she be?

Grabbing his phone with the intention of texting Mia again, he noticed three texts from her that he hadn't noticed. They must have come through in a spotty cell coverage zone on the way here. Quickly he read them. The first was an apology for her reaction this morning, which made him smile, but she went on to say she was waiting for the fire chief. Then she intended to head back to Nelson's.

He frowned with worry chomping through

him. What had happened? Why had she left before the fire chief arrived?

The third text read that she'd had a change in plans and wanted to meet him at Xander's. She'd put the address in the text.

A mix of relief that she was safe and jealousy that she'd reached out to Xander knotted in his gut. Despite Mia's confidence in her friend, Nelson didn't trust the man. He was too wily. Shrewd, even. And possessive of Mia. He tried to push aside his dislike for the man, but there was something off about Xander that raised alarm bells.

Nelson brought up Xander Beckman's address on the GPS and headed in that direction, then he called Jodie Chen. "Were you ever able to do a background check on Xander Beckman?"

"Yes, sorry, I've been swamped and just got the report."

He grimaced. "Can you give me the lowdown on him?"

"Yes, sure. Let me bring up the information," Jodie said. He heard the clicking of keys on a keyboard. "Xander Beckman left Dillon and attended California State University Sacramento. He graduated with a business communications degree and went to work for Full Freight Trucking, a small company operating up and down the I-5 corridor. He worked his way to manager and was employed there for several years before going out on his own. He bought into a transportation company, Transport and Trucking Unlimited, LLC, working as their CEO."

Nelson's heart stalled. Trucking? Transportation? His mind flashed back to the large grill of the semitrailer truck that had nearly run him, Mia and Diesel off the road near the reservoir dam. If it hadn't been for the runaway ramp, things could've ended very badly. Had Xander been driving that truck? "Who are his partners?"

"Oh, you'll like this," she said. "Ron Davies has a share of interest in the business. Along with two other Dillon natives—Andy Walsh and Kyle Long."

He remembered Mia saying that Kyle had been the one to coax her out on to the dance floor at the warehouse party. Were the four friends the ones who'd started the fire and framed Lindsey and tried to frame Mia? How?

Xander was supposedly Mia's friend. Nelson recalled all the things she'd said about Xander getting upset with Lindsey interfering in Mia and Xander's friendship. Had he been jealous enough of Lindsey to try to get rid of her? But he'd hurt Mia in the process.

And then Xander had left town as soon as he'd graduated high school, leaving Mia behind to face the town of Dillon by herself. Mia had said

Xander had only recently returned to prepare his family's property to sell. And they had become buddies again, going fishing, hiking and camping together.

Had Xander learned that Mia was investigating the warehouse fire and was he afraid she'd discover the truth?

But she'd done as good a job as any law enforcement investigator and still hadn't discovered any evidence to point to Beckman. Only suspicions of Andy Walsh and Kyle Long, because they'd lied about seeing her and Lindsey with the butane canisters and Ron Davies because he was trying to put her out of business.

At this point all Mia or Nelson had were suspicions. Until he had concrete evidence, he wouldn't make any accusations.

"Can you find out where Andy Walsh and Kyle Long are?"

"Already have that info," Jodie said. "Walsh is an accountant in Southern California, divorced. Kyle Long is a high school administrator in upstate New York. Married, two kids."

"Would you verify they are at their respective places and get back to me?"

"Of course."

"I'm headed to Beckman's place now. Mia might be there," he said. "I'll call with an update." He clicked off and turned down a gravel drive toward a house tucked back from the road and surrounded by forest.

As he approached Xander's family home, a warning instinct tripped down Nelson's spine. He parked and climbed out, keeping the door open as a shield in case he met gunfire from the house. When nothing happened, he rounded the back and let Diesel out, putting him on a long lead. "We have to find Mia."

Diesel lifted his nose, then looked at Nelson. The dog wasn't trained to track humans. But Nelson hoped that if the Lab caught Mia's scent, he would lead Nelson to her.

Was she here? In the house? Or the big barn off to the left? Or the small shed over on the right. Where was Xander's pickup?

He approached the house first, knocking loudly and announcing himself. Nothing. The only noise he heard were the birds in the trees. He went around the porch, peering in through the windows. The furniture inside was covered by white sheets and layers of dust. The place looked uninhabited.

Diesel strained at the end of his lead, pulling toward the shed to the right. Heart hammering, he let the dog lead him to the structure where Diesel sat staring at the door. The dog alerting and his own suspicions were a probable enough cause for him to push open the unlocked shed door.

Inside was the normal, though old and rusty, landscaping equipment one would find in a homeowner's shed. But on a shelf lining the walls were cans and cans of butane. Much more than any one person should ever have. Sitting in a box on the bottom shelf were more timing devices.

There was little doubt in Nelson's mind now that Xander Beckman was the one trying to kill Mia. Did he have her right now?

Withdrawing his weapon, he led Diesel to the large barn. The door was padlocked. But there was a window set high in one wall. He'd seen a ladder in the shed. He and Diesel rushed back to the shed, and he carried the ladder to the barn, leaned it up against the side just below the window.

Quietly giving Diesel the stay command and knowing the dog would obey, Nelson climbed up and peered through the window. He didn't see any signs of life, but he did see the semitrailer truck that had tried to run them off the road and Xander's silver pickup. Where was Mia?

Diesel let out a menacing growl. Nelson shifted on the ladder to look over his shoulder and froze as his gaze met Xander Beckman's.

The man held a gun aimed at Diesel.

"Tell your dog to back off," Xander commanded from his place at the corner of the barn.

Nelson gritted his teeth, his hands tightening

on the rungs of the ladder. Anger smoldered in his chest. He was surprised he didn't burst into flames. "Diesel, sit."

The dog sat, though he continued to emit a low growl.

"Xander, I'm coming down off the ladder. Do not shoot." Without waiting for a reply, Nelson placed his feet on the outside rails and slid to the ground. His gaze met Xander's again. This time the muzzle of the gun was aimed at Nelson's chest. But Nelson had no doubt the other man would shoot Diesel. Where had Xander been hiding? Where was Mia?

"Put down your weapon." Xander gestured with the gun at Nelson's holstered firearm. "And your phone."

He hated to comply, but Diesel stood in the line of fire between him and Xander, making the perfect target. Nelson withdrew his weapon, making an exaggerated show of holding it by the grip, and his phone from his pocket, setting both on the ground at his feet. "Where's Mia?"

Ignoring the question, Xander said, "Walk toward me."

Nelson walked a few feet forward so that he was standing next to Diesel. "I'm going to grab his lead." Slowly, keeping his hands in view, he bent and picked up the leash, whispering to Diesel, "You'll get your chance."

"Start walking." Xander's tone echoed with irritation.

Nelson bit the inside of his cheek to keep from snapping at him, then took two steps forward, Diesel staying at his handler's side. In a measured tone, he asked again, "Where's Mia?"

"Oh, you'll see her soon enough," Xander said, waving them forward more. "It just depends on whether she'll see you dead, or alive?"

Regret tore through Nelson. He should've told Jodie his suspicions about Xander being the one threatening Mia. He took solace in the knowledge that the Rocky Mountain K-9 Unit knew he and Diesel were here. When he didn't turn up or report in, they would come looking. But would they arrive in time? Or would they find three dead bodies?

His heart twisted. Nelson needed to keep Xander from shooting him or Diesel. Or from hurting Mia. He sent up a quick prayer for help and protection.

"You've been behind it all," Nelson accused, careful to keep his tone even. "From the beginning. You started the warehouse fire, didn't you?"

Xander smirked. "Do you want to know why?"

"Oh, I know why," Nelson said. "You've been obsessed with Mia since you were a teenager. And you decided pinning the fire on Lindsey would give you Mia, only you goofed up and Mia was blamed as well."

Surprise crossed Xander's face, followed closely by annoyance. "You're much more perceptive than she is. She had no idea. And it wasn't me who made a mess of things."

Interesting. He had a partner? Ron Davies? "Mia has a pure heart," Nelson said. "She sees the good in people. She needed your friendship. She trusted you and you betrayed her."

"I betrayed her?" Xander barked out a rough laugh. "No, she betrayed me. She didn't pick up on the cues. I kissed her. And she laughed."

Nelson raised his eyebrows. "If Mia laughed, it was because she hadn't been expecting or wanting your attention."

Rage shined bright in Xander's blue eyes. "Her loss. And now yours, too."

Pulse pounding an erratic beat, Nelson had to keep the man talking. But how long before Jodie sounded the alarm? "How did you start the fire at the warehouse?"

"It was pretty ingenious, if I say so myself," Xander boasted. He scuttled sideways and circled around behind Nelson and Diesel. Nelson pivoted as well, keeping the man in his sights.

"Move it," Xander said. "To the house."

Was Mia inside? Nelson complied, taking restrained steps when all he wanted to do was run to the house to find her. "Where is Mia? Tell me she's okay?"

Behind him, Xander snickered, a distinctly disturbing sound coming from the man. "Now who's obsessed with Mia?"

"I am," Nelson admitted. "Not obsessed. But I'm in love with her."

Saying the words aloud brought a fierce ache to his heart. Would he have the chance to tell her? Would they live long enough to forge a future together? Or would Xander succeed in harming Mia? In killing them all?

"Isn't that just too bad," Xander sing-songed. "Well, maybe not so bad. You get to end your days together. That's more than most get. Keep moving."

Xander's words brought both terror and relief. Mia was alive, but Xander had plans to do away with them both, just as Nelson suspected. No way could Nelson allow Xander to win. Glancing over his shoulder, Nelson said, "Then you shouldn't mind telling me your ingenious plan of starting the warehouse fire and how you got away with it."

"It was quite easy," Xander said, baring his teeth in a macabre grin. "All I had to do was convince Mia to bring her camp stove. I made her believe it was her idea." He rolled his eyes. "To pop popcorn." He snorted. "She is so naive. As if anybody wanted popcorn when they could have alcohol or drugs."

Nelson's fingers curled into fists. Mia would be devastated when she learned that she'd been a pawn in Xander's scheme. "But that doesn't explain how the fire started. She didn't use butane."

"No, she didn't, but I did," Xander crowed. "I brought several small canisters. I placed them beneath the pallet where I directed her to put the camp stove, again making it seem like her idea. The cans were open, filling the insides of the pallet with compressed gas. Then I had Kyle coax Mia away from the stove and away from *her*." The inflection in his tone on the last word was filled with loathing.

"Her, being Lindsey." Nelson didn't really need the clarification. Mia had already told him of the animosity between the two.

"Of course. She was standing in the way between me and Mia." Xander spat on the ground. "The plan would have worked if Lindsey hadn't gotten sick from the fumes."

"But you had no way of knowing when the canisters would explode," Nelson said, pointing out the flaw in his plan. There had been no timing devices found in the aftermath.

"Oh, I wasn't relying on the cans I'd hidden," Xander said, his voice full of arrogance. "No, as soon as Mia left with Kyle, I had Andy distract Lindsey long enough for me to put an open butane canister right next to the camp stove. Then I called Andy off and we walked away." His lip curled. "She should've stayed there, attending to the popcorn."

"But she didn't," Nelson pointed out. "She went outside before the butane exploded." No wonder there was so much fire. "Instead of one big canister, which had been the theory, you used several small ones."

"Yes," Xander chortled. "Our bumbling police department had no clue that I'd removed a bunch of the remnants, leaving only the ones that would incriminate Lindsey."

"How did you get Lindsey's fingerprints on the butane canister remnants?"

"I'd sent away for a fingerprinting kit." Xander's tone, dripping with pride, grated on Nelson's nerves. "I took one of her discarded soda pop cans, lifted her print and transferred it to the butane canister. Easy-peasy."

Nelson was sickened by Xander's pride in framing Lindsey. "Then you played the hero by trying to rescue the mayor's son."

Xander chuckled. "Yes. That's me. The hero."

They were almost to the house now. Was Mia inside somewhere, tied up and unable to move? Was she unconscious? Even alive? His stomach twisted. No, Xander said they would end together. She had to still be alive.

Or was Xander lying, giving Nelson a false hope?

SEVENTEEN

No! Nelson refused to contemplate Mia's demise. There would be no point in Xander playing with Nelson. Would there? If Mia were already dead, Xander would have killed Nelson on the spot. He held on to the hope that she was alive, and that God would see them through this ordeal. Together.

Needing to buy time, Nelson continued to probe Xander for answers. "How did you manage to get the confession note onto Lindsey's computer?"

Xander's eyebrows shot up. "What makes you think I did that?"

"Who else would have?" Nelson played to Xander's vanity. "Who else was smart enough?"

Xander's pleasure emanated from his eyes. "You're right, nobody but me could've done it."

Nelson stopped and waited as Xander moved past him and Diesel. Nelson kept his gaze curious, while at the same time putting pressure on

Diesel's leash, bringing the dog closer to heel rather than out front protecting him. Once Diesel was beside him, Nelson stepped slightly in front of Diesel and calculated the distance between him and Xander. Still too far to launch an attack on the man.

"Tell me how you did it," he prompted Xander, at the same time giving Diesel the hand motion to stay in place while he took a step toward Xander.

Xander's lips curled in a sneer. "She thought she was so much better than me. She thought she was better than everyone. But look at her life. A drunk for a father and a mother who escaped into oblivion with pills and dark shades."

Xander's expression radiated hate. "After the police questioned me and let me leave the scene, I broke into Lindsey's house and into her bedroom. Her computer was just sitting there on the floor." He snorted. "She thought she was being fancy with her password, but I knew it. She didn't realize I'd overheard her and Mia one day talking about it." He rolled his eyes and said, *"bestfriendsforeverM&L."*

That explained why there was no evidence of anyone hacking or spoofing the computer. It had been done the old-fashioned way.

Xander began to walk sideways toward the side of the house and Nelson kept pace, with each step inching closer.

"Who told you Mia was investigating the warehouse fire?" Nelson asked.

Xander shook his head. Something resembling sadness crossed his face, but the look was grotesque on him. Nelson doubted the man had any depth of feeling beyond that of his own self-interest.

"She brought this on herself. She started poking around," Xander said. "Asking questions. Andy Walsh's mom called Andy with the interesting bit of gossip that Mia was poking around in the terrible old case. Andy then called Kyle, who then called Ron, who called me."

"The three of them knew what you were doing and were okay with you setting the warehouse on fire?"

"It's good to have minions," Xander said. "Except Ron didn't know. He's so dumb. He couldn't even get his business up and running. I had to help him with it."

"But Andy and Kyle helped you."

Xander shrugged. "It was Andy who put the canisters of butane in Lindsey's car."

"Andy and Kyle told the police they saw Lindsey with the butane canisters," Nelson pointed out. "I thought your plan was to hurt Lindsey so you could have Mia to yourself, but you ended up hurting Mia."

"I couldn't help if the cops wanted to pin it

on Mia too because she brought the camp stove. The police assumed she was guilty by association. That's why I had to write that confession note on Lindsey's computer." He shrugged. "In the end, Mia got off."

"And still, she didn't want you." Nelson shouldn't take such pleasure in voicing that truth.

Xander's lips curled. "No, she didn't."

"You went off to college, never dreaming you'd come back here. But then you heard about Mia's investigation and returned."

"She wouldn't listen to me when I told her she needed to let it go. I hoped if I scared her enough, maybe she'd back off." His lips twisted. "Instead, you showed up."

It was a good thing he had. Nelson could only imagine what this man was capable of. "You shot at her cabin. With that gun, I take it?"

Xander looked at the weapon in his hand, then back to Nelson. "Just to scare her. I didn't even break the windows. I was doing her a favor."

The man was really warped to believe not breaking out the windows of Mia's home was a kindness. "And you cut her brake line."

That day unfolded through Nelson's mind. Now he knew why Xander's silver pickup had niggled at his mind: he's seen Xander drive by when Mia had crashed. Checking on his handiwork, no doubt.

"Yes, I did that because I was afraid if she kept badgering Ron, she'd learn I was behind the negative online reviews."

"You attacked us in the shed and then set her dock on fire," Nelson pressed. "Tried to run her over with one of Ron's pontoon boats and tried to run us off the road with your semitrailer truck. But since none of that worked, you set her cabin on fire."

Xander's eyes glittered with triumph. "Yes, to all. Aren't you clever. And now you will join Mia and you two can live out your final moments together." His gaze flicked to Diesel. "And him."

Chest constricting with dread, Nelson asked again, "Where is she?"

Xander moved to stomp his foot on a wooden door in the ground on the side of the house that Nelson hadn't noticed before. A muffled cry came from within. Mia!

Relief and dismay twisted in Nelson's stomach. She was alive but trapped in a cellar. Nelson took another step forward, releasing the leash in his hand, letting it drop to the ground. He prepared to launch himself at Xander, intent on overpowering him. The idea of rendering the man unconscious shouldn't be so appealing.

Then Nelson would rescue Mia and she'd get her heart's desire, her friend's exoneration. He'd use all the resources the FBI had to make sure

Lindsey was released from prison. Then Mia would be free to live her life. And he could only hope she'd include him in that life.

With a knowing chortle, Xander raised his other hand and wagged a finger at Nelson. "No, no, no. You think you can take me down and rescue the damsel in distress? Not today, Officer."

Xander lifted his hand higher and gave a short wave. A shot rang out, echoing through the trees. Dirt spurted up near Diesel. The dog flinched and Nelson spun, scanning the tree line. Someone was out there with a rifle trained on him and Diesel. Andy Walsh? Or Kyle Long?

Frustration bubbled, nearly choking Nelson. He held up his hands as a powerless rage washed over him. "I'm not going to do anything stupid."

"That's right," Xander said. "You aren't. I'm in charge here. Not you. You make one sudden move, your dog is dead, then you."

Xander reached down and undid the lock holding the cellar door closed. He pulled the door back, revealing a dark hole. He moved sideways, waving with the gun. "Inside, now. Both of you."

With another glance over his shoulder at the tree line, Nelson pointed to the opening. "Inside," he told Diesel.

The dog looked at him for a moment with uncertainty. Nelson gave a chin nod toward the cellar. Being the obedient dog he was, Diesel moved to the opening and sniffed, then quickly disappeared down a short flight of stairs into darkness. A happy whine emanated from the interior of the cellar.

Mia's soft tone floated on the air. "Diesel!"

Nelson's heart slammed into his chest as emotions flooded his system at hearing her voice. Relief, fear and love. How was he going to get her out of this situation? He eyed Xander. The man didn't even realize he'd put himself in the line of fire.

Readying his body to tackle Xander, Nelson was about to lunge when the man said, "Don't. I'm standing between you and the shooter, is what you're thinking, but how do you know I don't have more than one rifle at the ready?"

Xander looked off to the left, toward the woods at the front of the house. Nelson followed his gaze. Sunlight glinted off a scope high in a tree.

Nelson let out a frustrated breath and gritted his teeth. The guy was smart, he'd give him that. "You won't get away with this."

"I already have." He chortled and gestured to the cellar opening. "Your turn."

Nelson descended the stairs into the black pit. He had to crouch as the door slammed shut, beaning him in the back of the head. Pain reverberated through his skull. Darkness enveloped him.

On his hands and knees, he crawled forward. "Mia?"

"Here, Nelson." Mia's voice called to him from a dark corner.

As his eyes adjusted to the meager light eking its way into the cellar through the gaps in the slats of the hatch door, he found her and gathered her close. "Did he hurt you?"

"Not badly. But could you undo the duct tape? My shoulders are in agony."

He made quick work of ripping away the tape binding her hands and ankles. "You were right, Xander, Kyle and Andy framed Lindsey. Ron was just a clueless pawn in Xander's scheme."

She gave a long sigh of relief as she rolled her shoulders, then she took his face in her hands and brought him close. "Good to know. But what are you doing here? I asked God to keep you safe, not bring you here."

He smiled, glad to hear her feistiness. Loving the sensation of her strong, capable hands on his skin. "I prayed God would allow me to find you and rescue you," he stated, then dropped his forehead to meet hers. "Xander sent me the address to lure me here. But this is not much of a rescue, I'm afraid." Nelson was unable to hide the self-recrimination in his tone.

"Nonsense. You came. I can't tell you how much

that means to me. My hero." She pulled him in for a kiss.

Their lips met, hers soft but not tentative. She tasted of tears and hope. His heart clenched with love and fear and everything in between. His arms encircled her, drawing her ever closer, despite how awkward it was within the cramped space. But it didn't matter how uncomfortable the position, she was alive and safe for now. And he'd give everything to keep her that way.

Diesel let out a series of frantic barks. The hairs on the back of Nelson's neck rose in alarm. He tore his mouth from Mia.

Diesel pawed the ground and let out another series of barks.

A tidal wave of dread choked the breath from Nelson's lungs.

"What's happening?" Mia asked, the fear in her voice unmistakable.

"He's alerting." Nelson didn't have the heart to tell her that Xander intended to burn them alive.

"Alerting." The word ricocheted through Mia's mind. "As in he's detecting an accelerant?"

Nelson released her and moved to the stairs. "Yes."

A shiver of terror coursed over her flesh. She'd been right in assuming Xander planned to burn down his parents' home. With her, Nelson and Diesel trapped inside the cellar.

Diesel whined. She reached for him and hugged the dog close, her heart folding in on itself.

Not long ago she'd wanted Nelson and Diesel gone from her life. She'd wanted to keep them safe by banishing them, but no one had listened and now their lives were in imminent danger because of her. No, not her. This was on Xander. The man was out of his mind with wickedness. How had she never seen the evil behind his facade?

Nelson's big body blocked the slivers of light coming through the slats of the wooden door, but she could make out his silhouette as he rammed his shoulder against the hatch, the sound making her wince as he continued to throw himself at the hatch over and over again.

"Stop!" she said, unable to stand it, knowing the damage he was doing to himself. "You're only going to hurt yourself."

He let out a harsh growl filled with frustration and anger that matched her own. He shuffled around and used his feet to kick at the door but to no avail.

"I can help." She crawled to the stairs. "Let's try kicking the door together."

She maneuvered herself so that her feet were pressed against the hatch, back braced on the stairs. She kept her chin tucked to her chest and rested her head on the dirt floor. The edges of the stairs dug awkwardly into her spine. Nelson squeezed in beside her in the same position, his body pressed close.

"On three we kick," he said.

"Okay." She readied herself. *Please, Jesus, let this work.*

"One. Two," he said.

Before he could say *three*, a loud bang rent the air, shaking the earth and raining small debris down on them.

Shocked, she tensed. "What was that?"

Nelson put his mouth close to her ear. "Xander blew up his house."

A roaring noise beat against her eardrums. "What is that sound?"

"Fire!" Nelson shouted. "Ready. One. Two. Three!"

They both kicked at the hatch door and kept on kicking until the weatherworn wood finally began to splinter. A rush of smoke invaded the cellar.

"Keep kicking," Nelson yelled over the sounds of the blaze outside the confines of what could very well end up being their coffin.

Coughing against the acrid smoke burning her eyes, nostrils and lungs, she kicked with all her might. Her legs quivered with exertion, but a sense of urgency and self-preservation had her using every ounce of strength she possessed.

A slat in the hatch split completely. They continued kicking until another slat gave way.

Nelson put his hand on her shoulder. "Move aside."

She scrambled off the stairs and into a crouch beside Diesel, while Nelson used his hands to rip the slats apart, making an opening. "Mia, climb out."

There was no way the opening was big enough for him to squeeze through. Mia didn't want to leave him behind but knew the only way she'd be able to save him was to get out of the cellar and find something to pry the hole in the door wider. She joined him on the stairs, so close his breath stirred the short hairs at her temple.

"Be careful," he said. "Xander may still be out there. Take Diesel with you and get away from here. You can send someone back for me."

"I'll be careful," she promised. But there was no way she was leaving him behind.

She poked her head out. Thick smoke obscured visibility. *Please, God.*

Holding her breath, she wiggled through the opening, the rough edges of the broken slats snagging on her clothes. Kneeling at the opening, she helped Diesel squeeze through the opening.

Pulling her shirt up over her mouth and nose, she shouted to Nelson, "We'll be right back."

"No! Go. Get out of here," Nelson's voice battered at her.

Ignoring his command, she crawled away from the opening with Diesel belly-crawling beside her, until the smoke thinned and she could assess the danger. Dark smoke and flames roiled out of the shattered windows. The front porch blazed, the flames licking at the dry wooden structure the same way it had with her cabin. No doubt, Xander used the same sort of accelerant. She stifled a cough, afraid to alert anyone to her presence.

At the end of the driveway, she could make out three bodies watching the blaze. Xander and who else? She didn't have to think too hard to guess Andy and Kyle. Why hadn't she realized they had worked together to frame Lindsey and to try to shut down Mia's investigation? It made perfect sense. There was no way Xander could have pulled it all off alone.

Scrambling backward, praying she and Diesel weren't seen, she grabbed Diesel's leash, got to her feet and ran in a crouch through the dense smoke to the wood pile. The haze from the fire made it difficult to discern anything. She held her hand out, searching until she found the stack of wood. She groped the logs, until she finally found the ax. She dragged it through the smoke back to the cellar. Her eyes watered uncontrollably and her lungs burned.

"Nelson," she called into the hole.

"Mia! I told you to get out of here," he called back. He coughed, the sound rough.

"Move back," she said and lifted the ax to chip away at the remaining boards of the hatch. The smoke stung her eyes. Her breaths came in shallow puffs. Dizziness threatened but she couldn't stop until she'd made enough space for Nelson to get through.

"Mia, stop!"

She stilled and lowered the ax. "Can you get out?"

Then he was there, pulling her into his arms. She clung to him as relief coursed through her veins, making her weak and strong at the same time. She loved this man and was never going to be without him again. She prayed he held the same love and affection for her. She didn't know what she'd do if he didn't.

"We need to get away from the fire," he said against her temple.

"Xander and his cronies are out front," she told him.

The echo of gunfire pierced the air and a bullet slammed into the ground at her feet.

Taking her hand, Nelson tugged her to her feet. "Run!"

EIGHTEEN

The sound of pounding feet behind them and the possibility of another, more accurate shot being fired urged Nelson to a faster pace. He had to protect Mia and Diesel. He had to get them to a safe place so he could double back and disarm the men chasing after them.

With one hand gripping Mia's hand, and the other Diesel's leash, he raced with them for the forest grove of mixed conifers and aspen. The thick sagebrush growing between the trees would provide cover. The smoke thinned with every step, exposing them to their pursuers.

Beyond the roaring noise of the inferno that had once been Xander's family home, the distinct whine of sirens rent the air, bringing the hope of help.

Shouts behind them shuddered through Nelson, but the voices were too indistinct to make out the words.

Nelson pulled Mia behind a tree and tucked

Diesel between them. "I need you to just stay here," he told her.

Her teary eyes widened. "What are you going to do?"

Determination heated his blood. "I'm going to take care of Xander."

"But there's three of them." She grabbed a hold of his arm. "You can't take them all on. Not by yourself."

Her concern for his safety crowded his chest, making him ache. "I just need to keep them away from you until help arrives."

"You'll get yourself killed," she insisted. "I can't allow that. Let's go deeper into the forest."

Her words lodged themselves deep in his heart, right where his love for her burned brightest. He smoothed back her hair and cupped her cheek. "My brave little warrior. You'll be safe here. Diesel will protect you."

"Wait. I have to tell you something." Her voice took on a desperate plea.

He touched the tip of his index finger to her lips. "Hold that thought. I want to hear it. But time is of the essence."

He removed his finger and dropped a quick kiss, full of promise, on her lips. Then he took off, moving swiftly to the left through the trees, intending to come up behind the three men.

He needed to end this once and for all.

* * *

Mia leaned against the tree, trembling with fear for Nelson. Diesel sat on her feet, as if somehow rooting her to the spot.

She touched her lips where Nelson's kiss lingered and sent a prayer heavenward for his protection.

Diesel growled, a low vibration deep in his throat.

Mia crouched and hugged the dog close. "Quiet now."

She heard voices not far away. She hunched her shoulders, hoping to make her and Diesel as invisible as possible.

"This is ridiculous," a gravelly masculine voice said from just beyond the tree line.

Though the man's voice sounded familiar, she couldn't be sure exactly who the speaker was. Andy or Kyle?

"We have to find them," Xander insisted. Mia feared his knife-edged voice would be burning in her memory forever, the stuff of nightmares. "The two of them are the only thing standing between us and prison."

"Then we should have taken them out when we had the chance," another voice said. "But no, you had to toy with them."

"Stop your bellyaching," Xander said. "Spread

out. We have to get to them before they can get the police here."

"But he *is* the police," the first, gravelly-voiced man groused. "And can't you hear those sirens? They're getting closer. I say we run for the Canadian border."

"Great plan," the other voice said. "We're out of here." The sound of the two men running away filled Mia's ears. Like rats abandoning the ship.

"Cowards," Xander shouted.

Mia held her breath.

Footsteps drew closer and closer to Mia and Diesel's hiding place.

Too afraid to move, but fearing Xander was going to find them, Mia braced herself, ready to spring into action to defend herself. She unhooked Diesel's leash but held onto his collar.

The noises of a scuffle and grunts had Mia silently gasping. She peered around the trunk of the tree in time to see Nelson and Xander grappling on the ground. Nelson must have tackled Xander.

Mia whispered into Diesel's ear, "Go help your partner." She let go of his collar. The dog raced forward out of the trees, barking and snarling. Mia pushed away from the tree trunk and looked for something to use as a weapon. Seeing a small, sturdy stick, she grabbed it and ran to help Nelson.

The two men rolled back and forth in the dirt,

seeming to take turns getting the upper hand. Diesel growled, and his powerful jaws snapped at Xander.

Nelson had Xander flat on his back. Xander's hand groped around his boot, extracting a silver blade.

"Watch out! Knife!" she screamed.

Nelson rolled away and popped to his feet. Xander lumbered to his own feet, swinging the knife in an arc, barely missing Nelson.

Mia ran forward and struck Xander from behind with her stick. He spun, slicing the knife through the air. A sharp sting startled her as the tip of the blade nicked her arm.

Diesel lunged, his teeth sinking into the hand holding the knife. The dog shook his body back and forth as if wanting to tear the limb from Xander.

Xander screamed obscenities as he tried to tug himself free.

Nelson tackled Xander to the ground, then gave Diesel the command to release. Nelson jerked the knife from Xander's bloodied grip, flipped him onto his stomach, and pulled his hands behind his back, pinning them in place with his knee.

Nelson looked up at Mia. "The leash."

Understanding his intent, she ran back to where she'd left Diesel's leash near the base of the tree. Grabbing it, she darted back and handed the long, thin cord to Nelson, who wrapped it around Xander's hands, binding them together. Then Nelson tugged Xander to his feet.

"The others got away." Mia told him what she'd heard.

"They won't get very far," Nelson assured her.

Noise around them raised the fine hairs at Mia's neck. Smoke billowed as the fire Xander had set continued to consume the small house, and the shifting wind swirled the acrid cloud around them. Still gripping the stick, she moved to stand next to Nelson, holding the piece of wood up as a weapon.

Three dogs and two men and a woman materialized from the haze of smoke to greet them. Along with Kyle Long and Andy Walsh, their hands handcuffed behind their backs.

Mia breathed a sigh of relief when she recognized Sergeant Tyson Wilkes and his partner, the striking Dutch shepherd she'd seen in his office, and Lucas Hudson with his border collie, from the Rocky Mountain K-9 Unit. Mia didn't recognize the woman and her fierce-looking Malinois.

"Thought you could use some help," Tyson said. "But it looks like you have things in hand."

Nelson grinned. "You did help by not letting those two escape."

"Figured we better detain them and ask questions later," Lucas said.

The woman with dark hair pulled back at her nape stepped forward with her dog. "We'll take him."

Nelson relinquished his hold on Xander to the woman. "Thank you, Daniella."

Xander struggled against her hold, but despite his size he was no match for the solid and strong woman with ebony eyes that glittered with anger. Her dog emitted a rumbling growl that had Xander's eyes widening and settling down.

"How did you know to come?" Nelson asked Tyson.

Tyson met Mia's gaze. "Your friend, Lindsey, put up quite a fuss at the prison, insisting you had been kidnapped and needed help from the Rocky Mountain K-9 Unit. When the warden called, Jodie knew immediately you two were in trouble."

Mia sent up a prayer of thanksgiving for Lindsey's fortitude in making sure someone listened to her and to Jodie for acting so promptly.

"We'll meet you at the road," Tyson said, giving Nelson a pointed look that left Mia confused. He led Kyle away.

Lucas chuckled as he steered Andy to follow.

Daniella gave a chin nod toward Mia. "See to her wound." Then she dragged Xander to his fate. The fire department arrived and worked to put out the burning house.

Nelson turned to Mia, his eyes widening. "He cut you."

She glanced down at the blood dripping from the small nick in her arm. "Barely." She peered at him through her lashes. "But if you want to play doctor, I'll let you."

His mouth tipped upward at one corner. "Would you be a good patient?"

Meeting his gaze directly, she said, "For you, always."

He grabbed the sleeve of his shirt and ripped it at the seams. Carefully, he used the material to wrap around her wound. Then he pulled her close. "All I want from you, Mia, is the rest of our lives."

Her heart thumped in her chest. Hope and love expanded until she could barely take in air. She pulled back to search his face. She needed to be sure. "You do?"

He gave a decisive nod. "I do." Uncertainty flashed across his features. "That is, if you want to spend the rest of your life with me?"

Her heart flooded with all the bone-deep caring, admiration, need and adoration she could ever hold for this man who had played the superhero, the protector and her greatest love. "I want that, too. I love you, Officer Nelson Rivers of the Rocky Mountain K-9 Unit."

"And I love you, Mia Turner, PI extraordinaire."

Their lips met in a kiss that rocked her to her core. She couldn't wait to spend her whole life exploring ways to kiss Nelson.

Diesel wedged himself between them as if he wanted in on the embrace.

Laughing, Mia reached down to scratch the dog behind his ears. "We could never forget you, Diesel. You are a true hero." She smiled at Nelson. "Did you know he'd attack like that?"

"We've only done bite work once with Lucas in the suit," Nelson said. "Diesel jumped on him and licked his face."

Mia chuckled. "Well, he did great today."

"When it came to protecting his people, he was all in," Nelson stated, his gaze meeting hers.

Warmth spread through her at being included as one of Diesel's people.

Nelson tucked Mia against his side. "Let's get that cut looked at properly. And then we'll see about freeing Lindsey."

Mia's heart melted. "How quickly do you think it can be done?"

"We'll use all the resources of the FBI to expedite her release."

That was more than she could ever have hoped for.

Three days later, Nelson drove Mia to the women's correctional facility. It seemed that with the backing of the FBI, statements from both Mia and Nelson, confessions from both Kyle and Andy, as well as pressure from the state's attorney general, the county district attorney had no choice but to concede the error of convicting Lindsey for a crime she hadn't committed. A judge agreed.

Today Lindsey would walk out of prison a free woman.

Jazz music played from the SUV's radio and Mia was content. She was going to give up Jem's Rentals and move to Denver, where she planned to renew her private investigator license. She'd already negotiated the sale of all of Jem's equipment to Ron Davies, despite her dislike of the man.

Though Ron and Xander had been friends, and Ron had invested in Xander's company, and Xander had invested in Ron's rental company business, it turned out that Ron had had nothing to do with the warehouse fire or any of the threats against Mia. He was pompous and full of himself, but he wasn't a criminal. It had all been Xander.

Andy and Kyle had been charged for the warehouse fire along with conspiracy to commit murder for their part in trying to burn Mia and Nelson along with Xander's family home. Xander had been charged with murder, arson and multiple counts of attempted murder.

All three would see the inside of a prison cell soon enough.

On the radio, the announcer's voice broke into the music. "This just in. We've heard from a reliable source that the FBI have an anonymous witness placing William 'Hawk' Hawkins at the scene of the murder of Congresswoman Clark. Stay tuned for more at the top of the hour."

As the music resumed, Mia said, "That's a good thing, right?"

Nelson nodded. "If the witness is credible. Then yes, it could help convict the congresswoman's murderer. That and the forensics."

She held back a scoff, not wanting to dwell on the past. There was only room for the future. A future with Nelson. Her heart gave the little bump she'd grown accustomed to when it came to the man seated next to her.

The irony that Nelson had shown up on her doorstep suspecting she was involved in one crime, which she wasn't, but then stuck around to prove her innocent of the warehouse party fire and provide her protection against Xander and his buddies, wasn't lost on her.

Recalling his initial suspicions had her asking, "Hey, did you ever find the wig made from my donated hair?"

Nelson shook his head. "Not yet. But the Denver metro police are working closely with the FBI and the K-9 unit to find the wig and the person who set Kate Montgomery's car on fire."

"Poor Kate." She sent up a quick prayer for Kate. "Do you really think there's a missing infant?"

"No way to know until Kate wakes up," he replied as he flipped on the blinker to turn into the women's correctional facility. "But the team has been looking into every possible clue or lead that might explain why she had a car seat in her vehicle."

Mia hoped the woman would regain consciousness soon and shed some light on the mystery of who had hurt her and why.

Nelson parked near the prisoner exit and all of Mia's focus centered on the fact that Lindsey was being released.

After releasing Diesel from his compartment, they headed for the waiting area. Ten minutes later, Lindsey walked out wearing the jeans and sweater Mia had sent for her. Her dark hair was held back in a low ponytail and she was thinner than Mia had ever seen her, but she was smiling.

Heart squeezing tight with relief, Mia rushed to hug her friend close. Tears sprang to Mia's eyes. She'd finally done what she'd promised—exonerated Lindsey.

After a long moment, Lindsey drew back, tears of her own sliding down her cheeks, and then turned to Nelson. "Thank you. For keeping her safe. And for all you've done to help me."

Nelson smiled. "It was our pleasure."

Lindsey looked down at Diesel, who sat staring up at her with his broad yellow head cocked and his big brown eyes warm. She squatted down and looked the dog in the eye. "I hear you're a hero, too."

"We're all heroes," Mia said, proud of all they'd done to get to this moment. "And we all have bright futures waiting for us."

Lindsey stood and gave a nod. She lifted her chin and squared her shoulders. "I can't wait."

"I do have one question for you," Mia said with a sly smile.

Lindsey arched an eyebrow but stated, "You can ask me anything."

Taking Nelson's hand in hers, Mia grinned. "Will you be my maid of honor at our wedding?"

Lindsey grinned back. "Of course. How soon are we doing this?"

Mia looked up at Nelson.

His soft smile was filled with love. "This weekend."

Lindsey rubbed her hands together with glee. "That doesn't give us much time to plan. We better get started."

Mia laughed, her heart full of love for Nelson, Diesel and her best friend. She thanked

God above for sending Nelson to her cabin in the woods. Without the Rocky Mountain K-9 Unit, she wouldn't be here celebrating justice finally being served.

* * * * *

Don't miss Ben Sawyer's story,
Ready to Protect, *and the rest of the*
Rocky Mountain K-9 Unit series:

Dear Reader,

Thank you for coming on this journey with Mia and Nelson as they worked together to find out who was trying to hurt Mia. And in the process, they learned the truth of a crime from long ago and righted an injustice. Though a totally separate crime brought Nelson to Mia's door, it was the catalyst for them to fall in love.

These two had very different backgrounds and different motives for why they were afraid to risk their hearts for love. Mia's guilt for having a seemingly good life while her friend was in prison kept her from allowing love in, while Nelson was afraid of being betrayed as he'd been by his ex-fiancée. But ultimately, love won them over, softening their hearts and breaking down their walls. They have a bright future together.

I hope you will continue to read the Rocky Mountain K-9 Unit series. There are several mysteries to be solved over the course of this continuity. Who set the car on fire? Was Kate Montgomery the target? Is there a missing child? Who killed Congresswoman Clark and why? What will the investigation into the training incident reveal? And who killed the hiker, Emery Rodgers?

Until next time, may you be blessed with love, peace and joy.

Terri Reed

COUNTRY LEGACY COLLECTION

EMMETT
Diana Palmer

COURTED BY THE COWBOY

THE RANCHER AND THE BABY
Marie Ferrarella

Cowboys, adventure and romance await you in this new collection! Enjoy superb reading all year long with books by bestselling authors like Diana Palmer, Sasha Summers and Marie Ferrarella!

YES! Please send me the **Country Legacy Collection!** This collection begins with 3 FREE books and 2 FREE gifts in the first shipment. Along with my 3 free books, I'll also get 3 more books from the **Country Legacy Collection**, which I may either return and owe nothing or keep for the low price of $24.60 U.S./$28.12 CDN each plus $2.99 U.S./$7.49 CDN for shipping and handling per shipment*. If I decide to continue, about once a month for 8 months, I will get 6 or 7 more books but will only pay for 4. That means 2 or 3 books in every shipment will be FREE! If I decide to keep the entire collection, I'll have paid for only 32 books because 19 are FREE! I understand that accepting the 3 free books and gifts places me under no obligation to buy anything. I can always return a shipment and cancel at any time. My free books and gifts are mine to keep no matter what I decide.

☐ 275 HCK 1939   ☐ 475 HCK 1939

Name (please print)

Address   Apt. #

City   State/Province   Zip/Postal Code

Mail to the Harlequin Reader Service:
IN U.S.A.: P.O. Box 1341, Buffalo, NY 14240-8571
IN CANADA: P.O. Box 603, Fort Erie, Ontario L2A 5X3